USA TODAY BESTSELLING AUTHOR
Dale Mayer

HEROES FOR HIRE

TYSON'S TREASURE: HEROES FOR HIRE, BOOK 10
Dale Mayer
Valley Publishing

ISBN-13: 978-1-773360-55-3
Print Edition

Books in This Series:

About This Book

Welcome to Tyson's Treasure, book 10 in Heroes for Hire, reconnecting readers with the unforgettable men from SEALs of Honor in a new series of action-packed, page turning romantic suspense that fans have come to expect from USA TODAY Bestselling author Dale Mayer.

Tyson lost his wife and child several years ago, and he knows it's time to move on... So when his wife's best friend barrels into his new life and he finds out she's in trouble – as in serious stalker trouble – he steps up because he owes it to his late wife. Only he quickly finds out he wants to be at Kai's side – any way he can.

Kai has wanted Tyson for so damn long, but from the first moment her best friend saw him first, the two were like a lock and key. When Kai sets her eyes on him for the first time in years while doing a demonstration for a new training program her company developed, she realizes her feelings haven't changed.

But her life has changed, and she has a huge issue she doesn't want anyone to know about. After all, she's got a badass skill set... She can handle a stalker on her own... right?

Or maybe not. As the two delve deeper into the Kai's troubles, they find out things are much more complicated than they seem – and much more deadly.

Prologue

TYSON MORGAN SAT in front of the compound's dining room table. He hadn't seen such an incredible collection of men and women in one place since he had left the military. He never expected to see them in the private sector.

Levi spoke up. "Everyone, this is Tyson. He and Jace will be joining us."

Tyson glanced at Jace. They both turned to look at Michael.

Michael shrugged. "Hey, I said this was a good place to be. You've trusted me before. Trust me now."

"We wouldn't be here if we didn't."

Michael smiled. "Then take it easy and relax."

A beautiful woman walked toward them and handed them empty cups. She pointed to the coffeemaker on the sideboard. "Go ahead and help yourself."

Tyson glanced from the coffee to her. "Thank you."

She beamed at him. "Don't worry about those guys. Every one of them has a really ugly bite. But the only bite you'll get is if you're on the opposite team."

Jace snickered. "Hopefully we're all on the same team here."

"We are. We've been lucky," Levi said.

Just then Stone's voice wafted through the house. "Vehicle approaching."

Levi stood and took a look out the window. "Good. She's early."

"It's Kai." Ice chuckled. "What did you expect? Kai has never been late for anything in her life."

Michael asked, "Kai? That's a very unusual name. I've only known one person with that name."

Jace and Tyson turned to look at Levi. "The weapons instructor?"

"She's private now. Working for her own development company. But, yes, she's coming here to discuss some additional training."

Tyson felt a stir of interest inside. Which was an improvement over everything being just plain dead for so long. He had walked away from the military after his ideals had been shattered at the betrayal of several SEAL buddies of his. He hadn't had anything intrigue him in a long time. Even coming here hadn't been a decision on his own as much as it had been following Jace and Michael. But Michael had been a large part of it. If this place was good enough to bring him out of retirement, then maybe this was where Tyson belonged too.

Kai ... Well, he remembered her as being a small dark-haired dynamo who could put a man in his place in seconds. Not just by her tone of voice since she was military all the way. Not one of the men would've crossed her. She held their respect and their admiration. And he knew more than a few guys who gave her the top spot in their wet dreams.

He glanced at Michael and saw laughter in his expression. Mercy, Michael's partner, kissed him on the cheek. Michael wrapped an arm around her and tucked her up close. They were new in town. Apparently they were purchasing land together, building a place right next to the compound. Not a bad idea. There was some confusion about Mercy's future, except for one part of it—she was firmly attached to Michael.

Tyson didn't know what that felt like. He'd been alone for the last two years—since he'd lost his wife and child. His life had taken such a downward turn that he didn't know which way was up anymore. He just put one foot in front of the other because that was what he needed to do. But his heart hadn't been in it for a long time.

He'd have been lost without Michael this last year.

The door burst open, and the same dark-haired dynamo he remembered well strode inside, her grin flashing. "Good morning, all. Ready for a fun morning?"

Her gaze roamed from one to the other, almost mentally counting them off, adding names, judging and assessing. When she turned and studied Tyson, she said, "Hello, Tyson. How are you doing?"

She'd been his wife's best friend when they were growing up. And the pain just never seemed to end. He nodded his head. "I'm doing great. You?"

She tilted her head to the side as if seeing the lie for what it was. "You aren't doing great. You are doing barely okay. You're still in survival mode." She rubbed her hands together. "And that's a good thing because I came here to kick somebody's ass. You're it."

Chapter 1

TYSON REACHED FOR a towel and wiped his face. He had to appreciate the huge weight room and open floor space Levi had built here. The new room to the side he didn't understand yet but heard rumors that was part of Kai's visit. Speaking of her, he'd been tossed, thrown and stomped by some half-pint demon female.

Kai hadn't been kidding when she'd said she was ready to kick someone's butt.

Only now she was up against Ice, and that wasn't turning out the way Kai had planned. Tyson was handicapped with his moral code about hitting a woman. He knew it was also about skills, but he'd been unable to hit back as hard or as mean as he would have if he'd been up against one of the guys.

That had just pissed her off more.

He was who he was though, and Kai had been his wife's best friend. No way would he hurt Kai.

Particularly not a woman he knew he could hurt. Now if she had been a terrorist holding a semiautomatic rifle on them, maybe. Well, no maybe about it. But he could no more hurt Kai or any of the women in this place. And he knew that, for all Kai's skills, he was still physically stronger than she was.

The women might get mad and feisty and rib him over

it. But the men understood. Tyson had yet to see any of them battle with Kai and come out winning the match. But Ice ... Now she didn't have the same issues. And she was giving Kai as good as Kai was giving her. Matter of fact, it was a hell of a fight. He admired the skill the two women had so equally worked for so they could unleash it on the ugliness in the world. As he thought about that, his heart filled with sadness. He'd spent his lifetime trying to heal and help, but every time he turned around, another war was going on somewhere else.

Much like his history, he liked to remember little else. Tracy was an entirely different story. Memories of her were painful, but still he smiled at the thought of her. Kai's presence had stirred up the more difficult memories.

Kai had been very special to Tracy. And he'd always honored that. For the longest time he hadn't thought Kai even liked him. Her abrasiveness showed whenever he was around her. He never really understood it but just accepted it. Tracy, on the other hand, used to laugh and say he had Kai all wrong. And she'd get over it. Whatever *it* was.

"And she did ... eventually," he muttered under his breath.

One of the guys beside him turned to look at Tyson. He shrugged and wiped his face. He had no idea what Kai was doing here. But, so far, she'd had a round with everybody. He was all up for any kind of martial arts training, but that couldn't be exactly what she was here for. She was a weapons instructor so, unless she brought some new toys, he didn't get it. How come she'd left the military? He'd sworn she was a lifer. Then life changed for all of them, him included. As he looked around the room at all the people here who left the military, he realized how normal that was. Now Kai worked for a private contractor. Why had she changed careers? And what was she doing here?

He grabbed a bottle of water off the counter and took several gulps. A round of cheers and clapping behind him had him turning to see Ice and Kai shaking hands—both tired, sweaty and glowing with triumph.

"A draw?" he muttered, not that it mattered both women were bad ass.

Kai grabbed a towel, wiped her face, tossed it around her neck and said, "Now that we got all that out of the way, let's take a look at some of the new toys."

Behind her she pointed at a rolled-up mat. "Rhodes and Merk, you want to roll that out for me?"

They grabbed it and, with a startled grunt, managed to drag it to where she stood.

She laughed at the surprised look on their faces. "Yeah, it's heavy as it has a special resistance to it. Lay it down for me, will you?"

They stretched it out.

"Now walk across it to me."

They walked across, shrugged their massive shoulders, turned and walked again. "Feels like a normal mat."

She nodded. And then held up a remote in her hand. "Not quite." She clicked the button and said, "Now walk across it."

The two men exchanged glances but stepped onto the mat. They had to forcibly lift their legs off it to take another step. They stared at the mat, then back at her. Rhodes asked, "What the hell is that?"

"A new kind of platform so you can adjust the amount of resistance during a workout." She handed him a thick leather belt. "Put this around your waist."

She waited until he had it buckled in place, then pointed at the mat. "Drop and give me ten."

Rhodes hit the floor and bounced up. By the second push-up he was swearing. By the third push-up the swearing had turned a whole lot nastier.

Kai chuckled. "I'll lower the resistance. Now try again." Instantly he could do push-ups.

"Now watch," Kai said as she turned up the dial and Rhodes strained harder. "Now this." She turned the dial right to the end. Even with everybody cheering him on, Rhodes couldn't get his chest off the ground.

"What the hell magic is this?" Merk roared.

"No magic about it. It's a torture instrument," Rhodes snapped. "You want to turn that all the way back down again please?"

With a chuckle Kai turned the knob down. "New special magnets on the inside affect your energy. It creates a stronger gravity pull. Think about how much weight you have to use when you're powerlifting or doing machine work. This is resistance training at a whole new level. These mats, plus adding one or more of these"—she lifted smaller ankle and wrist bands—"will help you get more out of your workouts." She turned to look at the fascinated faces and grinned. "It'll make a huge change to the way you work out."

Back upright, Rhodes took off the belt and handed it to Levi.

Levi shook his head. "I already know what these things can do."

Rhodes handed it off to Michael as he strapped it on, this time with Merk holding the remote for practice. He sat up. "I wouldn't have believed it. These things are deadly."

"Sure, but it'll also build and tone muscle faster, stronger, better than ever before."

Michael grinned. "But at what cost? Our egos are not so easily replaced."

Kai chuckled. "Maybe, but I do have a new virtual-reality set for you to try out."

Murmurs hummed through the room.

Tyson wondered. He hadn't seen anything like that yet, but he hadn't been here more than forty-eight hours. He glanced at his buddy, looking back at him. Together the two men shook their heads, raised their eyebrows and focused again on Kai.

"This one is for target practice. We have specific VR programs which Levi is working on in the training room. What you have at the moment is the option of three training programs, which we will hook you up to. I can show you one of the programs right now. This one is nice and simple. I would like a volunteer." She glanced around and said, "Tyson, you're up."

He stepped forward obediently, wondering why she was picking on him. She fitted him with the headset and gave him a belt plus what looked like a futuristic pair of gloves yet a realistic-looking weapon—only it was plastic with some weight behind it. And, instead of ammunition, it had a control panel on the side. He stared at her and said, "I don't even play video games, so this will be totally new for me."

"And while you're playing," she said, "we have a monitor for the others to see what you're seeing. But you're in the middle of it. So let's just do this as a test run." She turned to Levi. "Did you get the installation completed?"

Levi nodded. "Yes." He motioned everybody to the back of the room where a clear wall separated Tyson from the rest of the crew. He turned and glared at what appeared to be a ten-by-twelve space. What the hell that meant he didn't know.

Kai's voice came through some kind of a speaker system in his head. "Okay, Tyson, not to worry. This will just be practice. Hit the button on the left-hand side of your belt."

He hit the button and was on a slum street in a North American city. He turned slowly, stunned at the details showing up around him. There even appeared to be total interaction as a newspaper floated aimlessly in the wind in front of him.

"Tyson, you understand this program is just a simple training program to help you work on target practice, response times, cognitive discernment and a host of other things. So get ready."

Suddenly out of the corner of his eye, he saw a motorcycle rip around the side of a building, the driver with a gun in his hand who shot off a round. It wasn't that Tyson took a hit physically. But it was almost like he had. In fact, the scene around him went static instead of dynamic.

"That hit was a kill shot. You'd be dead in reality. You have two options. You can switch the settings. The entire scene disappears, and you're back to the empty room, or the scene freezes. Why these options? One allows you to walk away, ending the game, maybe answer a phone call—whatever the situation. The other allows you to consider the scenario and assess performance. Now if you'll stand back up ..." Kai stared at him.

Tyson shook his head and realized he was down on the ground. His body had reacted as if he had taken a shot. He glanced at the odd gloves to see sensors flashing on his system.

"Now we'll run that again. This time it's up to you to

decide if you take the hit or if you can shoot somebody."

Within seconds a motorcycle came toward him. He raised his gun and fired. The motorcycle spun out of control, flashed past him with the driver rolling to the side. Tyson didn't know if it was a direct hit, but, considering the guy still held his weapon, Tyson realized he would be a target if the man survived. Tyson raced to the alley and watched. The motorcycle driver didn't make a move. Just as Tyson thought it might be safe to step back out again, another motorcycle came from the opposite direction. The driver screamed, "Asshole, that was my brother you just killed."

And bullets hailed in his direction. For the next ten minutes he executed evasive maneuvers, firing shots to keep the gang from taking his life. By the time the program ended, Tyson was shaking, his adrenaline running through him, his body covered in sweat.

The glass wall slid to the side. Kai walked in, reached up and unbuckled the headset. She studied him. "How are you feeling?"

With his chest heaving and his breath coming out in rasps, he nodded. "I'm fine, but that's quite a rush."

She grinned. "It is."

"Did you have anything to do with that invention?" he asked.

As she unbuckled his gloves and the belt and took the weapon away from him, she answered, "I didn't do any of the technical work. But I was in on the testing from the beginning."

He walked to the other side of the room, a big grin on his face, and for the rest of the morning watched as everybody had a chance to try out the new system. He turned to Levi and said, "That is a hell of a training program."

Levi nodded. "What we can't ever do is get soft. We can't ever lose that edge that keeps us who we are in the field. So, yes, it's a big financial investment, but then I'm investing in our lives. And that's what counts the most." Levi slapped Tyson on the shoulder. "You did a good job in there. Welcome to the team. It's good to have you." And he turned back to the others.

Tyson wasn't exactly sure how to take that because, as much as he really enjoyed what he'd done this morning, it still wasn't the same as understanding what life here as part of the compound would be.

Michael walked over. "That's a hell of a deal Levi's got going."

"I can't argue with that. Perhaps this is where we belong."

"I'm positive."

"Yep, you've made a home for yourself. I still feel like an odd man out."

"And you will for a while. No doubt about it. But these are good people. Don't forget that there are all kinds of people. Just be glad to know that others like us are out there."

"Are they like us? Have they had the losses, the tribulations, the trials, the agony?"

The smile fell away from Michael's face. "Yes, they have. Every last one of them."

Tyson studied his buddy's expression for a long moment and then nodded, something settling deep inside. "Good. Then maybe there's a place for me here too."

KAI WATCHED TYSON walk away. He'd done incredibly

well, considering he was the new boy on the block and she'd been picking on him all morning. She'd beaten the crap out of him, trying desperately to get him to hit back. But she'd forgotten about their code. Not only was it a case of not hitting or hurting a woman but also the fact they had his late wife between them. Tracy had been Kai's best friend since they wore pigtails and took tap dancing lessons as five-year-olds.

Tyson and Kai had both felt the loss when Tracy had died in childbirth, taking Tyson's daughter with her. And Kai knew that memory was between them at all times. Even when on the mat. He would always be someone who took it easier on her because of that relationship. And that was the last thing she wanted.

She wanted to kick him out of that fugue state he was in. Bring him back to life. Tracy had been gone for two years. It was long enough. It was well past time for him to get his act together and rejoin the land of the living. She couldn't believe it when she found out he was here with Levi.

It was a good thing. She'd heard Tyson had left the military. And, at the time, she thought that was the right decision. It was as if he had had a death wish. He took any and all missions, pushed himself to the edge, always just a hair past whatever, but he wouldn't let them see him lose control. As if joining Tracy was the only way he could see a future for himself.

It wasn't unusual in the military to see a reaction like that. Sometimes it went the other way with men getting freaked out and becoming too cautious. In other instances they became the opposite, as if daring fate to take them as well. She knew Tracy would be horrified if she saw how off the wall Tyson had gone after her death. He tried to launch an investigation into the hospital and the doctors responsible. There was possibly a case there, but Kai knew it wasn't in his best interests to keep focusing on it.

Tracy had died from complications during labor. She'd been at home while he'd been off on a mission, and she'd gone into labor three weeks early. He'd planned to be home with her, but she'd been alone, until the last minute when Kai arrived. By the time Tracy got the help she needed at the hospital, it was too late. Kai figured guilt had to be what had driven Tyson to that destructive edge.

He hadn't shared too much with the rest of his team. One of them flung him to the ground and sat on him until he could pound out of Tyson what the hell was going on. But even then they had treated him with kid gloves. But he wasn't left alone from that time forward. He wasn't going anywhere unless he was part of the buddy system.

She'd heard it happen before with other SEALs. She imagined it wasn't all that uncommon. Some divorced guys felt like their world came to an end. Other times, divorce was like a whole new life. Losing a loved one, well, that was harder than anything else. But when you blamed yourself, that just made it even worse.

Tyson was a good man. It had taken her a long time to see it. She'd been sure no man was good enough for her best friend. But maybe that was more of a cover so she didn't have to examine her own attraction to him. Feelings that appeared to be just as strong today. She sighed inwardly. She thought she'd stuffed all that away. But the sight of him, well, it was a sledgehammer to her heart, knocking down the wall she'd hidden behind.

He'd loved Tracy as much as Tracy had loved him. But it was too fast, their relationship. They were married within weeks. She'd been pregnant within that first month. Tracy never did things in a small way. She was flamboyant and passionate. Tyson probably had no idea what hit him. But the roller coaster ride had ended in disaster. Kai wasn't sure if he even understood just how much he'd been through.

"Kai, these are some awesome toys," Jace said.

She beamed. "Aren't they? I absolutely loved being part of the testing. I helped set up the scenarios, the settings, the weapons. That's my contribution to the research and design. And of course I'm now heavily involved in the marketing as I know many people in the industry. With the experience I bring to the table, it's easy to tweak these prototypes for all our benefit."

Jace nodded. "I never expected to see something as advanced here. Tyson and I have only been here a couple days. We came at Michael's urging. And of course, Levi's offer." He gave her a crooked grin.

She remembered some of the stories she'd heard about this man. Lethal. But picky. She liked that part of him. "Levi's done right by you," she said quietly. "I'm delighted to see Tyson here."

Jace slid a gaze toward his buddy and nodded. "It's good for him. Will hopefully give him a new lease on life."

"Doesn't look like he appreciates it much though," she said with a laugh.

"In truth, he hasn't settled in yet. He sits off to the side, alone, in spite of all the welcome, and just studies everybody and often leaves the first chance he gets," Jace said.

Kai turned to look up at him. "She was my best friend, but she was a hundred and fifty percent of everything to Tyson."

"And Tyson … he's a dragging-his-heels kind of guy."

"He still stepped up to the plate when it was about marriage and fatherhood."

"I always wondered though if it wasn't too fast for them," he said, his voice neutral.

She understood. "I had the same thoughts myself, but Tracy knew the minute she saw him and understood that was it. Everything else, as far as she was concerned, was wasting time."

Jace smiled. "I remember when Tyson first met her. He looked completely shell-shocked. But not anywhere near as much as he did after she died. He's never been the same again."

Kai stood, took a sandwich from one of the many platters Alfred had brought to them and said, "Tyson had to adapt fast to all that was Tracy. Then he had to adapt faster eight months later. But he's doing it. That's what counts."

Ice and Levi were having a heated discussion at the far side. Kai didn't know if it involved her or not; she hoped not. The items they brought in today were done deals. She just wanted to make sure Ice and Levi were happy. But Kai sure as hell believed in these items for training. She had a few more tricks up her sleeve, but she figured the men were pretty well worked out for now.

She glanced at her watch and winced. "I have to leave within the next hour or so. If anybody has any questions, maybe we can do an informal session right now." Instantly, she was surrounded.

"How many levels of difficulty?"

"How many more can you add on?"

"Can we change the weapons? Everything is different, depending on what weapon we have."

"Can we play this outside?"

And the questions kept coming. She laughed. "Okay, let's see if I can give you some kind of a fact sheet. There are handouts, but I know that's not the same as getting it from the horse's mouth. So, at the moment, there are three levels. However, within each level are several levels of difficulty for each scene. There are three current scenes—one in the woods, one in slums and one in an urban setting. We do plan to set up enemy lines, like behind terrorist lines. We also plan to set up one for a big city, as in skyscrapers, dealing with snipers. And we're contemplating other scenarios like Coast Guard settings."

She heard exclamations and murmurs over those suggestions, which made her smile. "I guess you guys like the new toy."

"It's freaking awesome," Stone said.

She always had a soft spot for the big guy. That he walked through life now with his supremely awesome prosthesis the same way he walked when he had a flesh and blood leg just made her admire him all that much more. Of course, the fact that he had a partner who appeared to adore him as much as he deserved would have gone a long way to making that adjustment easier for him. Kai glanced around the room and realized almost everybody was paired up.

A group of women stood to the side. She knew some worked in town. The place was just a happening community. She didn't know how Alfred handled it. What she had heard was one of the women now worked with him as well. Her thoughts pulled back to the men.

"Okay, as for weapons … you have several choices." She walked over to one of the large cases she had brought with her. Laying it on the ground, she popped it open. "We have a crossbow, a Beretta, an assault rifle and a police-issued service revolver. Now should you want or feel the need for other weapons, then let me know. We'll do what we can. We have to go through this whole process to set up a new weapon, but it's getting easier. I do understand though. Like you, I have favorites."

Stone asked, "How about a knife?"

She eyed him with surprise. "That's an interesting suggestion."

"We all carry them," he said. "But it's hard to get enough training using them."

She sat back on her heels next to her case and thought about it. "That'll be a whole lot more difficult." She tried to work it through in her head but couldn't imagine it herself. "I'll tell the design team and see what they come up with. You guys have my email, and I'll leave my business cards with you. Suggestions are always welcome. As you work your way through the programs and the levels of difficulty, etc., you can certainly send us whatever tweaks or suggestions you have. If you want to cuss us out as you're getting your ass kicked on a daily basis, we'd love to hear that too." At the snickers and snorts, she chuckled. "Honestly you're the guys this is for, so it'll be awesome to hear back from you about it."

Just then her phone beeped. She pulled it out, checked the number, and her smile fell away. She read the text. **What's your decision?**

She hurriedly returned her phone to her pocket and tried to regroup. She shouldn't even be here with this asshole tracking her constantly. She just didn't know whether he was serious or some kind of a screwball. She'd already contacted the police, and her company knew what was going on. She didn't want to involve anybody here. It wasn't her style.

Besides, she'd yet to find a situation where she couldn't look after herself. She wasn't about to start looking for one now. The guys had more questions for discussion, and then a good forty minutes later she escaped to her vehicle.

She got in and turned on the SUV engine as she spotted Tyson in the open doorway, watching her. Her heart picked up a few beats. Damn that man. Even now he looked lost. And yet, she doubted anybody else would see it. Then again he wouldn't appreciate anyone noticing. It had to have been a tough day for him. Even though she wished it wasn't the case, just seeing Kai would bring back memories of Tracy. Kai could only hope at this point they wouldn't be too painful for him.

But staying away hadn't diminished her feelings. After seeing him again, she figured nothing would. Hopefully he'd dealt with his loss because he'd had all the time he would get. She'd been waiting. She could only pray she got the chance to find out if what she felt was real or not. And if Tyson could feel that way for her.

The trouble was, somebody else apparently felt the same way about her.

Chapter 2

S HE DROVE BACK to headquarters and raced upstairs. She couldn't believe she'd spent so much time in this cement building. When she'd left the military, she'd wanted a job that didn't have her stuck in an office all day. And true, she did leave to meet people, but she was still here for many hours every day. Too many if she were honest. In the military she'd been a trainer and had spent lots of time inside and outside. "I got another one," she said in a hard voice as she strode across the open space.

The designers lounging on the far side staring at something on the monitors jumped to their feet. "Another one?"

"Yes. Another one." She pulled out her phone to show them the text. "See?" Her phone was passed from man to man.

"That's ridiculous. What does he expect you to say or do?" Tommy asked. His flamboyant color choices for his wardrobe did not detract from the fact that he still had more acne than most eighteen-year-olds. He was one of those genius teenagers. He'd been caught hacking government files at twelve because he really wanted to see if UFOs were at Area 51. It'd taken more than a hand slap to stop him. Once they got him designing new military training programs, he'd taken to them like he should've taken to school. Once he turned eighteen, he was part of this company. A lot of money was invested in their new programs, and they were always working on new designs. When she came on board, she'd insisted on shares. That had led to an investment program they could all live with.

Warren, who'd started the company, walked over at the commotion. "Did you get another text or was this one an email again?"

She nodded. "A text."

He shook his head. "Forward it to the cops."

"Like forwarding the last half dozen made a difference," she scoffed. It was irritating that the police had been unable to track the sender. Although Tommy, the in-house cyber-genius, hadn't had much luck either. He'd found the accounts were closed as soon as the emails were sent out. So finding the asshole would not be easy. Her stalker apparently had cyberskills she could only dream of. She'd take a fistfight over some sneaky cyberattack any day.

"Any idea what it's all about?" Tommy asked. "We set up several new walls and added an encryption to your email so he can't access that again. Surely you must have some idea of what's going on?"

She shook her head. "Wish to hell I did."

"How did Levi's team like the VR system?"

She could feel her face light up with excitement. "They were stunned."

Warren grinned. "Now that's what I like to hear."

It was one of the benefits she brought to the company. Connections. These guys started with an idea, and, with her help, they tested, trained and developed them. Now it was up to her to find buyers. Only so many people specialized in elite military training. Eventually they'd be in the gaming market, but right now it was all about training warriors to defend their own.

"Did you ask him about other markets?"

She shook her head. "No, not yet."

Warren's face fell. "We can't run without money."

She nodded. "Not to worry. I'm having lunch with Levi and Ice tomorrow."

Tommy's face was immediately wreathed with smiles. "That's Levi's lady, right?"

Kai nodded and kept her thoughts to herself. None of these guys were military. "She's his partner in life and in the company, yes." She remembered the beating she took at Ice's hands. Ice was a top-notch warrior.

"She's also a stunner," Warren said. "A hell of a good-looking woman."

Tommy said, "What's she doing with Levi? She should be here with me."

Warren snickered.

That brought a wave of raucous laughter from the other programmers. Kai shook her head at Tommy. "Ice would eat you for breakfast."

"She'll eat me for breakfast, and I shall eat her for lunch," he said with a smile, waggling his eyebrows.

Knowing he was just being one of the "guys," a behavior likely learned from Warren, she sighed. "I should teach you a lesson and bring Ice here."

Warren jumped to his feet again. "That wouldn't be a bad idea. I wouldn't mind meeting her myself." He rubbed his hands together.

Kai stared at the men around her. "You guys have no idea."

The thing was, they really didn't have any idea. They didn't understand how different Ice and the women in the compound were, the way they lived and showed others how to live. The compound was full of top-trained elite soldiers. Nothing less than the best would be acceptable for the partners. She understood most of the partners were weapons specialists and martial arts experts, although some she imagined weren't. But each one would have something special to bring to the table. They were special men. Not one would accept anything less. She wished to hell she belonged there. Something about that atmosphere—well, it made her homesick in ways she hadn't considered. They all had someone. They all belonged. And she wanted that for herself. She'd felt out in the cold for too long.

This stalker asshole was making the sensation worse. She felt increasingly isolated. The guys more laughed at it than worried about it. But, for her, a level of unease sat just under her skin.

Her future might be undecided, but every time she tried to think forward, this stalker asshole intruded. It was irritating. And scary.

What did he really want?

"TYSON, WHAT DID you think of the virtual-reality training program?"

He turned to Levi. "As somebody who hasn't played many video games, it'll take a little getting used to, but it was unique, different, and I think it has tremendous potential."

"I'm not sure gaming experience helps anybody with a training scenario like this," Stone said. "Our own real-life experiences are probably more helpful. I really like the idea of using different weapons. They all feel so different in your hands."

"They still have the same weight in VR as in reality." Rhodes studied the weapons on the table. "Looks like they've used the 3-D modeling program and then incorporated accurate weights to give us the same feel. It's not quite there yet."

"Maybe that's a good thing," Ice said. "We don't ever want to mistake these weapons for the real ones."

Levi chuckled. "Hopefully our men will never have the real weapons in the VR training room."

"We knew the room was being transformed into something, but nobody had any idea just what you two were up to." Flynn grinned at Levi. "You do know how to keep a secret. And that's damn near impossible around this place."

Levi shook his head. "Kai and I have been in discussions for the last year. But only about three months ago did I realize the prototype was to the point where they needed some real-life testing."

To Tyson it made complete sense. It also helped him understand how Levi had afforded this. It couldn't be cheap. On the other hand, the security company was doing incredibly well. The compound that had started with just four members was now massive. And still growing.

Bailey walked over carrying a tray. "Too bad Kai left. I have fresh cookies." Bailey smiled up at the men. "And if there was ever a way to a man's heart ..." She held out the platter. But before anybody could take one, Ice stepped forward and took the biggest. She chuckled at the look of outrage on Levi's face.

"I figured I'd better snag one before none are left," Ice said.

Stone snorted. "You stole the one I was going to take."

"I was after that one," Levi said in disgust. "It was the

biggest."

Her voice smug, Ice said, "Of course I only took one. You'll have a dozen. It won't matter if yours are a little smaller."

Stone nodded agreeably instead of answering because his mouth was full.

Tyson had to admit he was still unsure of everybody's names here. He knew most of the men personally. But the women not so much. There were a lot of them. Some worked in town; some worked here, and some didn't appear to do anything. But he knew they probably did; he just didn't know what their jobs were yet. He knew Bailey worked in the kitchen because she seemed to constantly appear with food.

Just then she stepped in front of him with the platter of cookies. He smiled and said, "Thank you very much, Bailey."

Her smile brightened. "You are by far the most polite man here."

That set off a tirade from the others. "The new guy is just sucking up so he gets more cookies," Logan said. "I'm leaving in a couple hours, so I should get extra cookies first."

Agreeing, Bailey held the tray out for him. Before Logan could reach for one, Harrison grabbed several for himself. "I'm leaving too."

Walking to the coffeepot, Tyson poured himself a cup and turned to look around at the wonderful camaraderie he was unexpectedly overwhelmed by. He'd never thought to see something like this. And that it was here right in front of him with people he knew. He wanted to join in, but, at the same time, he still remained on the outside.

Jace poured a cup for himself. "It's almost too good to

be true," he said in a low voice.

Tyson nodded. "Michael did tell us that."

"Exactly."

They'd trusted Michael for a lot of years. He hadn't let them down yet. It was a relief to know this time was no different. Somebody else's face kept popping into Tyson's mind. *Kai.* She'd been the same as he remembered her. Innovative, high energy and a dynamo. Tracy used to laugh and say Kai only had one speed, and that was overdrive. He'd seen her in action many times, and he had to agree.

But there'd been a change in her when she'd gotten that text. A disquiet settled on her face. That's when he'd seen the fine tremor in her fingers as she packed up. There was a lull in the conversation around them as everybody worked on their cookies. Into the silence he asked, "Did anybody else see Kai's expression when she got that text?"

A dozen heads turned toward him.

"I did," Ice said. "But it was subtle. You had to be watching her features when it happened."

Tyson nodded. "Subtle or not, that message worried her."

"Like us, she leads a full life. I'm sure some aspects of it aren't very nice," Harrison said. "I doubt it's man trouble though. She'd work anybody over who gave her one bit of conflict during her classes."

That brought out more chuckles and stories of Kai over the years.

Tyson couldn't let it go. "She looked afraid," he said in a low voice.

"How afraid?" Levi's voice was hard. "I didn't see her face. I was at the far side of the room."

Tyson studied his new boss. He knew Levi well; so did

many of the men here. He was a no-nonsense take-it-at-face-value type of person. Tyson knew he had to back up what he said.

"Very afraid," he said firmly. "Her face went white, and then she turned away. I saw her eyes. They were bleak and scared."

Levi turned to Ice.

Ice shrugged and said, "I saw something, yes. Whatever was in that text bothered her."

"But she didn't say anything so I doubt it was an emergency," Levi said. "It's not like she gave any kind of a physical response as in somebody close to her was in a car accident or something."

"No. It wasn't anything like that." Tyson thought back to the way she'd pulled out the phone almost hesitatingly, as if she didn't want to see what was coming. "It's happened before. And she's afraid it'll happen again."

Stone asked, "But what? What is she afraid will happen again?"

"I have no idea. But I don't think it's anything good."

Chapter 3

KAI WALKED INTO her apartment, tossed her gear and jacket where she stood. Her boots came off next, and, by the time she reached the bathroom, the rest of her clothing was off. She stepped under the hot shower and let it pound on her sore muscles. She no longer slept. She worked herself to the bone and filled every waking moment so she didn't have to think. When she did think, it just hurt and sent her stress levels off the wall. This was like the twelfth if not fifteenth text message she'd gotten. The messages were all the same.

Choose. What will you do about it?

She had no idea what the choice was supposed to be, what she was supposed to do something about. There was no looming question in her world. There was no conflict, no big issue. In the beginning she had tossed it off as being a wrong number. She responded after the second and third time to say he had the wrong person; go find somebody else to bug. But the emails hadn't stopped coming.

She shut off the water, and, using two towels, she dried herself as she walked into her master bedroom in her small apartment. When she'd left the military, she'd had her choice of what to do. She was accustomed to living in a small space and didn't really want to buy a big house. Besides, she wasn't into the family scene; she just wasn't there yet. Her apartment felt safer.

Which was stupid. She had great self-defense skills and had spent years instructing soldiers on the latest and best weapons as they came on the market. And here she was, slowly being eroded by text messages. She wanted to laugh at herself, but all she could do was cry. She always had a feeling of being watched. The sense of somebody keeping tabs on her. She didn't have any criminal background training, but any woman alive understood how dangerous a stalker was. How had he gotten her phone number? It didn't make any sense. Forcing herself to think of something more pleasant, her mind jumped to Tyson.

He looked like he was healing. Compared to when she'd last seen him, at Tracy's funeral, he looked fabulous. Then he'd been a broken man, which was to be expected after such personal losses. To land as part of Levi's group was huge. Here, he was still doing what he did best, helping people, and was with the team that he needed. It was interesting to see that Jace was with him. And Michael.

They'd all walked away from the military after one particularly bad mission. Several men had been killed—and the commander blamed. It came out eventually that somebody had deliberately sent them into action on bad intel to mess up the commander's record. The fallout had come too late to save the men—or the commander. It was just one more straw in the long line of straws that had disenchanted the men with their life and their mission. Tyson couldn't imagine the lives of the injured men of the one unit. Seven injured and one dead from that single unit alone. Then Michael himself had gone to ground for over a year. Not that she kept tabs on them. Hard to do when they were damn good at hiding.

But, in Tyson's case, she'd been keeping tabs on him since forever. It was all she could do. Besides, she'd promised Tracy to keep an eye out on him. When Tracy realized she wouldn't make it, she'd entrusted Kai with Tyson's care. At the time, Kai hadn't been able to protest. What was she supposed to say to a dying woman?

She had nodded, held her best friend's hand and promised to do anything to make Tracy's last few moments peaceful while she frantically wished for the ambulance to get here. Tracy had fallen unconscious fairly quickly after that while still at home and had died less than an hour later in the hospital. Kai had tried to keep that promise. Yet initially Tyson hadn't wanted anything to do with her.

She'd phoned and stopped by his place afterward, but he didn't answer his phone or door. She'd checked on him via their mutual friends for regular updates. She'd hated how he wouldn't talk to her. Apparently not only was he a wounded animal, long gone to ground to lick his wounds, but he'd also only seen Kai as a reminder of all he'd lost. How could she argue with that? For a long time she'd gotten up every morning apologizing to Tracy for not doing more.

Until Kai had finally made peace with herself and with the fact that Tyson had to walk his path. But that didn't mean she had to walk away. Now she just kept watch, even reached out and talked to Michael at one point. But after Michael left the military, she'd lost touch with him. She knew they were from California originally and now all lived in Texas, but that was all she knew.

Still, as long as Tyson was doing okay, it was all good. She knew Tracy would be sad to see how much Tyson had suffered, and she'd be the first to give him a swift kick up his butt, tell him to move on. She'd also be the first to cheer his progress. And he'd made a lot of that. At least from what Kai could tell. It was an easy thing to tell someone, but it was another thing to do it. As Kai knew herself.

Her phone went off again. She closed her eyes and pinched the bridge of her nose. She had no idea who the hell it was, but in her gut was a sinking feeling that she knew it was another one of *those* texts. She brought it up, glanced at it and read it out loud. "I know where you just were."

She sank slowly onto the edge of her couch and stared at the text. In a loud strident voice she spoke into the empty room. "Asshole! You're just saying that to unnerve me—or because you were following me." That would imply he knew her schedule. She ran through all the scenarios she could think of; every one of them was distressing. There had to be a reason why he tormented her. She just didn't understand. And she didn't quite know what to do about it.

Just then her phone rang. Startled, she almost dropped her cell. It was Warren from work. She could talk to him. "Warren, what is it?"

"I was hoping you could get me invited to that lunch tomorrow with Ice."

"Hey, it's more personal than business."

"You know how this works. It's networking. She's hot."

"It doesn't matter how hot she is. Levi would tear you to teeny tiny pieces and feed you to the crocs before he'd let anybody like you close to Ice." She tried to keep her voice light, instead of releasing the anger unfurling inside. "She's also not the type to like being talked about or spoken to in such a manner."

No way would Warren make the first cut with Ice. Hell, Ice didn't need Levi's protection, but, if Levi got wind this guy was panting after her, Levi would have something to say.

"You don't know that. Maybe she'd rather do business with me than with you."

His voice had dropped into a tone she'd only heard a few times, but each time she hated it. There was almost a sneer to it. Not somebody she wanted to work with. But she was in no position to buy them out, and neither was she in any position to walk away. "Enough of that. It's not happening."

"You just want to keep her for yourself."

"Ice is a good friend, Warren. It's not a matter of keeping her to myself. We go way back, and none of Levi's team knows you. This is also how business works."

The silence at the other end meant Warren finally understood he had gone too far. He sighed. "Sorry. You're right. I'm just frustrated. You get to talk to all the movers in the military world, and I'm stuck in the office."

Kai's eyebrows popped up. He rarely apologized. Even so, it was one thing for the guys to talk like that at work when she wasn't around, but she really didn't like the lack of respect when she was there. "Whatever. You still don't get to meet Ice." She hung up the phone. Then she leaned back and groaned. Warren was harmless. He was also irritating as hell. They all were in some ways. Tommy was okay, but he was at that belated teenage stage of whistling at girls as they walked by, making rude noises, telling body-function jokes. She kept hoping these guys would buck up and pull together to become the dream company she needed. The thing was, they had the components for an incredible set of equipment. Not just equipment either. The products they'd come up with so far were mind-boggling. And they were incredibly important for the military and for the people of Levi's team. She was glad she had a hand in getting them into the market, at least as far as the prototype Levi had.

Putting away her phone, she hopped up and dressed quickly then walked to the kitchen to put on some coffee. She'd had several cups at Levi's place. It seemed like she could almost inject the stuff for the amount of caffeine she needed on a regular basis. As soon as the coffee was dripping, she went to her laptop to check her emails. A friend—a stewardess who often stayed with Kai—wanted to know if she would be in town next month. She quickly answered that one, grateful this email was safe. Tommy at work had set it up. A couple were more business prospects. She responded the best she could. Most were just leads discussing products' availability times. She enjoyed this part of her job. She was excited about the new VR project they were developing, so it was easy to talk about, and that made it less sales oriented and more about relationships. Business relationships, those were good things.

The last three looked like spam, but they'd come to her priority inbox. She opened one so she could see the preview. And swallowed hard. It was a picture of her front door. The front door to the apartment building she lived in.

She sat up to see who it was from, although she knew the account would already be closed. She dropped her elbows to the table and leaned her forehead into her hands. Now the asshole knew where she lived. She wasn't sure she wanted to open the other two "spam" emails, but she'd never been the *bury her head in the sand* type of woman. She could more be counted on to be the goat that bounced off the cliff edge. Knowing she needed to check, she clicked on the second one, and sure enough there was a picture of her front door with her apartment number clear as day. "Okay, asshole. I see you know where I live."

The third one was a little more disconcerting. This message had a picture of her vehicle, her license plate showing. "You know where I live, and you can get at me any time," she confirmed out loud. She leaned back and thought about that. She needed to check her weapons again. It was something she did weekly. She had one under her pillow—her father's old service revolver from his years on the force. There was a shotgun in the closet that had been her grandfather's but she had no ammunition for it. She'd had no time or inclination. She'd really wanted to close the door on that part of her life.

Had in fact done just that.

She'd bought into the company and had hit the ground running. But she didn't have anything in the vehicle. It was time to think about carrying a handgun on her at all times. When she left the military, she'd stopped thinking in terms of weapons. And she'd been happy to walk away from that whole world. She'd lived it, breathed it and had been grateful to find something else to experience.

Although she'd been happy to walk toward something completely new, it had been an adjustment but she'd taken to it and never looked back. But it seemed like all she'd done was go from a global type of warfare down to a one-on-one combat. And there was no settling the sick feeling inside. She might have mad skills, but that wouldn't stop the asshole if his behavior escalated, and he did seem bent on coming after her.

She forwarded the three emails to the cops handling her case. Within minutes she got a phone call.

"This is Detective Mannford, calling about the three recent emails. You have any idea who sent them?"

"You always ask the same question, and I always have the same answer. No, I have no idea. And, if I did have an idea, you wouldn't have to ask me for his name. I'd have sent it along with the emails."

"They were sent to you about two hours ago. Actually, they were sent an hour apart from one another. You didn't see them earlier?"

"I avoid checking my emails when I'm in a business meeting. I was at Legendary Security for most of the day. I did get a text again while there. Then I went back to the office and then home, where I just found the emails." She frowned as she realized she hadn't checked her email at work either. She shrugged. "I guess I was a little on the scattered side. Normally I'd check my emails at work, but I didn't today."

"I doubt it makes any difference in terms of whether he would've only sent one or all three. I suspect it's just more to torment you. Were all the other texts exactly the same as the first one?"

"Yes, exactly the same. Except the last one." She quickly relayed that message and sent it. "I can forward those to you as well."

"Do that. We'll put them in your file."

"You had no luck tracing any of them yet, right?" She knew he hadn't. Tommy had tried. According to him, there was no way to track the sender at this point. He tried to explain how cell phones could be bought and dropped for minimal cost. Unidentified phones you could make a call on. There was just no simple solution. Tommy had said, "If somebody wants to be an asshole, they can be a really big asshole in this tech world."

Like she needed to hear that.

TYSON SAT DOWN at his laptop, opened up his email and worked on his opinion on the VR system. Like everyone else, he took his turn in the VR room. Each had found something that needed a little tweak. Tyson didn't know if his was important or not but figured the programmers would want to know. *There was a black spot when I turned to the left after I did a certain footing. I repeated it several times. Each time a block showed up. So I figured it was in the program code.* As he tried to explain it in an email he realized how foolish this was. He grabbed his phone, looked up Kai's number and dialed it. When she answered, her voice hesitant and quiet, he asked, "Did I wake you?"

"No, not at all." He listened as she cleared her throat and came back, apologizing. "Sorry. My throat is scratchy. Just going to have a sip of coffee here."

In his mind he could see her pick up her cup and swallow, her throat moving strong and vibrant as the rest of her. He was such a fool. He could still hear her say, *I was always one hundred percent. It's just Tracy was like a hundred and fifty percent. I always came off looking a little bit less when compared to my best friend.* When he had seen Kai today, she'd reminded him so much of Tracy. That same exuberant over-the-top love of life. And he wondered how he'd ever seen Kai as anything less. Sure, she'd been prickly at the beginning but then had warmed up. With Tracy around, he had seen the two women's similarities, but Tracy had always shone a little brighter for Tyson. But that was then. As he studied Kai now, he realized Kai was calmer. But still so damn alive. She was always on fire, always on top of the conversation. She spoke with an animated full-body approach. Whereas he was quiet, always sat off to the side, rarely spoke to her. But not Kai. She was the center of attention, and yet not because she needed the attention but more because everyone gravitated to such energy. He certainly had.

"Okay, that's better. Sorry about that," she said lightly. "What's up?"

"I found a glitch in the programming," he said quietly. "I tested it several times, and it showed up every time."

"Good, that's what we want to hear. Obviously we would prefer no glitches, but something like this will help us fix it. Where and what did you find?"

He explained the details.

"It didn't show up with any other foot patterns?"

"No, not that I could see. If I get a chance, I'll try again tomorrow."

"If you get a chance? Are you on a mission?"

"I'm leaving the day after," he said. "But the VR room is a little busy at the moment." He smiled in spite of himself as her laughter rang free, filling his ear and even the room. She had such joy for life.

"Now that is good to hear."

"Are you coming back?" he asked. Then instantly frowned. Why the hell did he ask that?

"Back to Levi's place? I'm not sure. I'm meeting Ice for lunch tomorrow."

"I'll be going into town with her. We have a lot of running around to do."

"You're coming for lunch?" she asked.

He analyzed her question for any hint of disappointment or upset, but, for the life of him, he couldn't tell. It was just curiosity. He wasn't sure if he should feel happy or sad. "Not sure what's planned. A shipment's coming in. She might meet you alone while we're all off doing other things."

"Well, if you join us, good. You're always welcome."

"Thanks. We'll see how the day goes." An awkward silence filled the space between them.

Finally she said, "I need to grab some food so I'll talk to you later."

"Will do." He hung up and stared at his cell. "What an idiot you are."

He leaned back and thought about it. Of all the people he might want to start going out with, Tracy's best friend was not likely to be the healthiest choice. But, as he started to realize, he may not have a choice. Because, so far, she was the only one he'd found an interest in. He knew the others would be worried. Afraid he wasn't really interested in Kai herself but was interested because he wasn't ready to let go of Tracy.

But he had done a ton of work on himself since he'd lost his wife. He'd seen a therapist for months—something he had never told anybody because it confirmed how he wasn't wrapping his head around what had happened. He'd been so angry, so very upset, and of course the guilt had been crippling. It had been the first thing his therapist had worked on. As the big one moved and shifted off to the side and became so much less, they worked on the next few things. He would never feel good about the loss, but now he could think about Tracy and remember her joy, not feel that haze of anger and frustration that come over him at her death.

"Tyson?" There was a hard knock on his door. Levi asked, "You in there?"

Tyson pulled open the door and looked at Levi. "I'm here."

Levi smiled. "A man of few words."

Tyson shrugged. He didn't understand the necessity for small talk.

"Mannford just contacted me from town. He wanted confirmation Kai was here today."

Tyson frowned. "Why?"

"Apparently she's having a potential problem with a stalker. She's received several emails and texts. One of the emails today said he knows where she's been."

"Did he give proof he knew where she'd been?"

"No, but he sent photos of her apartment's front door, her apartment number and her vehicle's license plate."

"Did somebody follow her here?"

"Ice is checking the security feeds right now."

"A tracker on her vehicle?"

"It's possible. Ice is meeting Kai tomorrow for lunch. I want you to take some equipment and check her car."

"Will do."

After Levi walked away, Tyson closed the door and turned back to his laptop. Stalker? Kai?

How the hell did that work? He ran through what he knew about stalkers and realized he didn't know enough. He turned to his laptop for more information.

When he sat back a half hour later, he'd learned one of the major problems with stalkers. Too often they escalated to something much worse. Thank God Kai was one hell of a fighter. She was a warrior woman in a tight spot, and she'd give hell to any man who tried to kidnap her, rape her or anything else. But she also was susceptible to bullets, and drugs knocked out anybody. Even her.

For the first time in a long time he started to worry about someone else. He realized that, if someone didn't help her, she could die too.

Chapter 4

PEACE OF MIND was required to get a good night's sleep. Feeling rough around the edges, Kai hopped into the shower just so she could wake up enough to start the day. A couple cups of coffee later and she was awake enough to figure out what she had on her calendar. She'd probably spend the morning in the office until meeting Ice for lunch. She glanced around her apartment and considered the emails she'd gotten. Maybe she should stop by the police station first. She didn't want to be forgotten or her stalker file to get thrown in a corner. Maybe if they saw her face every once in a while, they'd realize how much of a person she was, not just a file or case number. That didn't mean the cops weren't doing their job, but she felt so helpless.

When she'd had to deal with trouble before, she had a team beside her and orders to follow. And yet, here she was no longer part of the team, asking the police to step up and do the job her own unit would have done at her side. It felt odd and uncomfortable, and she admitted it made her feel insecure. In this new world nobody cared about her but her. At least not to the same extent. When she'd bought into the tech company, she'd been hoping it would become her new family. But then Mark had died in an accident, and everything had changed. Mark's death had ripped away her newfound sense of security, her sense of belonging.

While still raw from that, she'd struggled to regain her footing and to take the helm of the company without being overt about it. And then the stalker had found her. Outside of keeping watch for anyone suspicious, eyeing her cell, taking precautions, there wasn't a whole lot she could do about him. And therein lay the problem. She wanted a target. She wanted somebody she could go after. But there was no one.

The longer she thought about that, she'd be better off going to work an hour later and hitting the shooting range first. Her self-confidence had taken a hit with this stalker, and a surefire way of handling that was to regain control. She needed to be in control, not feel like a victim. Target practice was one of the best ways to feel empowered. Leaving the military she had also lost sparring partners. For the first time in a long time she realized maybe her skills weren't quite as good as they should be. She needed time on the VR system herself.

She sent Warren a quick text that she'd be an hour late to the office. She packed up and headed to the local range. She had a membership there and was one of the regular faces. As she walked in, Johnson gave her a wave. She signed the book and headed into the back.

He called out, "Bad morning?"

She laughed. "The worst but that's going to change."

And true enough, forty minutes later, having beat the crap out of the targets, her arm now on the weaker side but her sense of invincibility and capability up, she realized she could start the day again. She high-fived Johnson as she walked out. "It's all good now."

He shook his head. "It's a sick world out there. You watch your back."

She shot him a startled look, wondering if he understood just how true a warning that was for her. She realized it was likely a comment he'd have tossed off to anybody. She walked to her car, considered the photos somebody had taken of it. But found no sign of anybody here, nor any sign of damage. She lay down on the ground and checked to see if anything was obviously out of place or damaged or a threat to her. And found nothing. But did she know what the latest gadgets even looked like?

She should have asked Levi if somebody could run a check on the vehicle. But that would require an explanation, and she wasn't good at that. Everybody would say Kai was invincible. Nobody would dare attack her. She'd knock them hard if they did. At one point she had believed it to be true but the assiduous stalker's threats were like fine sandpaper grating against her self-confidence. And the result was ugly.

Back at the office she caught up on the paperwork dumped on her desk, answered email messages and waited for the rest of the crew to come in. When nobody did, she sent out text messages. **Is there a party I missed?**

After a few minutes Tommy answered, **You said we had the day off.**

She stared at the text in surprise. **I did? When?**

This morning. You said everyone's worked hard so take the day off. We all deserved it. So please don't change that now.

Her heart slammed against her chest. She hit the telephone icon to call him. When he answered, she said, "I'm not trying to be an asshole of a boss, Tommy, but I didn't send a text this morning."

There was silence at the other end. "You didn't?"

"I did not," she said firmly. "And, until my stalker problem is solved, everybody has to speak with me—personally—about each and every email and text supposedly from me. I have no problem with everyone taking the day off, but I wouldn't send a text to say that. That someone did scares the crap out of me."

"It should," he said, his voice serious. "It means the stalker knows your contacts. Great job."

There was condemnation in his voice as he said it. She gasped in surprise. "Hey, I told you about this a long time ago. So why are you blaming me?"

He groaned. "I'm not blaming you. It's just that he's gotten all the contact information on my phone too."

"Is that a bad thing?" She shook her head. She could handle a stray bullet, and most weapons and karate were a huge help for any hand-to hand defense. ... And of course she'd learned a lot of dirty tricks from her combat training. But damn this technology stuff was confusing as hell.

"If he knows what he's doing, it's definitely a bad thing. And so far he's demonstrated a decent amount of skill."

"Am I supposed to get a phone that can't be traced like he has?"

"That might be a good idea. We never considered it before because it didn't seem necessary. It's not like you're some model or some famous figure who'll have a fan following."

She sat back and reached up a shaky hand to her forehead. "Really? That's what you have to tell me? I'm not famous enough to have a stalker? So you think I'd make it up?"

"No, we definitely don't think that you've been lying. But, at the same time, I really had thought the guy wasn't serious. But now he's impacted my world ..."

She leaned forward and stared out her office door at the empty desk in front of her where Tommy would normally sit. "Oh, I see. So now that it's touched your world, you're ready to do something about it?" She winced at her own bitterness and gave herself a head shake. She wasn't given to fits of panic or flights of fancy. So what she really needed to do … was calm down. "Look, I can't talk about this right now. I'll talk to you later."

Just as she went to hang up, he said, "Wait."

She looked at the phone again and said, "What?"

"Do we still have the day off?"

She glared at the phone and hung up on him. To the empty room she said, "Wouldn't it be nice if he came in and helped me out?" She sat, wondering how her wonderful new start in life had turned to sawdust in her mouth. How the company, the job she really loved, had evolved into working with assholes overnight.

She knew Tommy was an arrogant hormonal teenager, but he never got to her like this before. It made perfect sense he wouldn't be worried about a stalker. He lived in innocence. Untouched by the darker side. To a certain extent, she did too. But the military had shown her what an ugly place the world was. Seeing what people did to each other … But it had never been personally directed against her. She'd never been singled out like she was now. And that was a whole different issue.

She could sit here and wait until her appointment with Ice, or she could do something productive. First she needed to check in with Warren.

"Why didn't Warren contact me when he got that text?" she said to the empty room. She hit his contact number and waited for the phone to dial. When it went to voice mail, she figured he must have gotten the same text about taking the day off from work, even though he was part owner of the company. She'd normally expect a lambaste phone call from him. Particularly after their conversation last night. Warren was cheap in so many ways, and giving the staff the day off wasn't something he'd do or agree to.

With nothing important in her emails that she couldn't push off for another day, she got up and headed to the open parking lot on the same floor and behind their second-floor offices. Very convenient and where everyone had one designated spot to park.

She walked to her car, stopped and looked around. She hated that sense of being watched all the time. And yet, she never saw anyone. Shrugging, she got into her vehicle and drove toward her lunch appointment with Ice.

The bank and the nearby restaurant where she was meeting Ice were both in the same small shopping mall. Her insurance company was in the mall too. She stopped there first and renewed her car insurance. While there, she made inquiries about life insurance. Armed with pamphlets, way more than she had any intention of reading, she left and headed to the bank. Business banking done first, then she took out some cash for herself. In this day of plastic, it seemed like nobody used cash anymore. But she still preferred it for some things.

In the back of her mind she was afraid her cards could be traced. If somebody was following her, they'd know where she lived by tracking her bank cards. She was tempted to just freeze them all. But instead, she took enough cash so she'd be fine for at least a week, then walked to the restaurant. Ice wasn't there yet. Kai ordered coffee and sat by the window. She had paperwork she could do in the meantime.

When a shadow fell on the table, she looked up and smiled. Only her smile faltered. "Hi, Tyson. It's good to see you."

"Are you sure?" he asked in a low tone. "It doesn't appear that way from the look on your face."

She shook her head. "That's not true," she protested. "I was expecting Ice. When I saw a man I didn't recognize initially," she admitted, "I got a little worried."

He slipped in the chair opposite her. "Worried? Is that because of the phone message that upset you yesterday?"

She stared at him, her mouth open. "What's that about my text message?"

He waved a hand, dismissing her protests. "I saw your face when the message came in. It's obvious whatever was in that text upset you."

She closed up her paperwork, shoved the files into the bag she'd brought with her and sat back with her coffee. "I don't know what you're talking about." Inside though she wondered, *Should I tell him?* She needed help from someone.

"You do know what I'm talking about, but, for the moment, you don't trust me, and you figure big bad Kai can handle any trouble coming by herself."

She snorted. "Everybody meets trouble they can't handle at some point."

"Have you got trouble you can't handle?"

Just then somebody approached the table. She looked up to see Ice and Levi. She frowned. "The whole gang is here too?" she joked.

Ice sat down beside her, boxing her in against the wall, and Levi sat across from her beside Tyson.

Levi said, "Detective Mannford called yesterday, wanting verification you came to the compound. We checked the security cameras but didn't pick up anybody following you."

Silence followed for a moment while Kai regrouped. In a small voice she said, "Oh." She stared out the window for a long moment, then turned back to him. "So he wasn't there?"

Levi shook his head.

Ice said, "We checked all the feeds from an hour before you arrived through the day and the night. No strange vehicles. No strangers. All was well on that score."

"Well, that's something then," Kai said with forced cheerfulness.

"Which leads us to believe there might be a tracker in your vehicle," Tyson said. He reached across the table. "Give me your keys."

"I checked but didn't find anything. That would explain some things though." She let out a breath, pulled out her keys and tossed them toward him. She watched as Levi stood up so Tyson could leave. When Levi sat down again, Kai glanced from him to Ice. "You must be wondering what this is about."

"Detective Mannford explained a little bit," Levi said. "Why don't you fill us in?"

"Wish I could, but I know damn little," she said. "I started receiving strange text messages." She pulled out her phone, brought up the latest text and handed it to him. "Read for yourself. Yesterday after I left your place, I went to work for a couple hours. When I got home, I found three emails. Each one showed a picture of my place. The first one showed a picture of the front of my apartment building. The second was a picture of my actual door. The third was a picture of my vehicle parked at my complex."

"So he's saying, *I know where you live. I know what you*

drive. I can come for you anytime." Ice's voice was cool but gentle.

Kai winced and nodded. "That was my take. I sent everything to the cops as I have done since it first started. I had a really bad night. Woke up this morning feeling shaky, went to the firing range, popped off a good few rounds," she said with a bright smile. "Felt better. Earlier I sent Warren a text, saying I would be an hour late, but he never responded. When I got in, the place was empty. I contacted Tommy, my whiz kid, and asked where the party was because apparently I had missed it, and that's where it gets a little more disturbing."

Levi and Ice leaned a little closer.

She continued. "Tommy said he'd received a text from me, saying everyone could take the day off, that the company was doing well, and they all deserved it." She sat back. "Of course he wasn't impressed when he found the text hadn't been from me." She groaned. "I tried to call Warren because he hadn't responded to the first text. I knew he would've had fits if he'd received a copy of the one about taking the day off, but I got no answer. I decided nothing needed to be done at the office, so I left to do some errands until lunch. I was doing paperwork when Tyson walked in."

Levi settled back. "Well, this does make for an interesting scenario."

Ice put it a little more succinctly. "Hell no. This is a shit storm."

WITH KAI HAVING coffee safely with Ice and Levi, Tyson went out to her car. He walked around the outside of it first, taking several photographs. He didn't know if she had bothered checking for any outside damage or not. He opened up the driver's side and looked inside. With all four doors open, he took his time using a bug detector to check for anything. He found nothing inside. He moved to the trunk, found it empty and carried on.

Underneath the vehicle he found what he was looking for. The vehicle had a LoJack tracker on it—an object common on rental vehicles for keeping track of renter's movements. He took several images, then left it in place. With the image on his phone, he walked back into the restaurant, ordered himself a coffee and sat down beside Levi. He held his phone out to Kai and said, "You're being tracked."

He watched the color wash out of her face. She sat back and swallowed hard. But so typical of Kai, she didn't panic or scream in outrage. She studied the image, gave a clipped nod and said, "I checked but didn't see that." She wrapped her arms around her chest. "I feel like I should have."

"It was well hidden. And at least you thought to look," Levi said. "This wasn't your field in the military. Plus we often can't see what's happening right in front of us ... Not until it's too late." His tone changed as he added, "Speaking of trackers, I need to see your phone."

With that she brought it out and handed it to him. There was silence at the table as Levi quickly dismantled her phone and pointed to a small dot on the inside. This time there was shock and anger on her face.

He quickly dropped it on the table. "You need to get yourself a new phone."

She stared down in frustration. "Why? The damage has been done."

"Yes. So he knows where you've been, what you are doing and how you are doing it. What we want to make sure of is that he doesn't know what you do from here on out."

"Who knew you were coming here?" Tyson asked.

"Warren. He knew about the meeting … and wanted to come with me. He's a bit of an asshole. But that doesn't make him a criminal."

Levi nodded. "Maybe not but it could make him a bigger asshole than you think."

She groaned. "I really don't like the idea of having to look at everybody in my circle of friends to see if one of them is a stalker."

"Chances are he won't be in your circle of good friends. A stalker is generally outside that intimate level but close enough to know who you are or where you work."

She nodded. "I understand. But that means he's in the realm of acquaintances. And I run a business with a lot of networking. I meet a lot of people. I have a lot of business contacts on my phone."

Levi turned the phone back on and copied the list to his phone. "I'll send these to you as soon as you send me a brand-new phone number nobody knows."

Tyson watched her face as she struggled to see just how much of her life would change now.

"Shit." She stared out the window. "I guess that's the first step."

"Your network of contacts should be checked out. But with your VR system, your company is on the verge of making it big."

She stared at Levi. "You realize how many men in the military would be in that group?"

"And how many of those contacts have IT experience?" Tyson asked. "How many of them had access to your cell phone?"

She swallowed. And shook her head. "Many have IT experience but access to my cell phone … not many at all."

"It's that 'not many' part the concerns us," Levi said. "We need names and the last time you saw them. And what type of relationship you have with them."

She took several deep breaths. "That'll take a moment or two."

Ice opened a bag at her side, pulled out a notepad and pen and shoved it toward her. "We're not going anywhere."

Kai gave her a grateful look. "Thank you but this isn't your problem."

"And that'll just piss us off," Tyson said, his voice low.

She shot him a hard gaze.

But he glared back. Like hell he would walk away when she was obviously in trouble. Not his style. He already knew it wasn't Levi and Ice's style. He also knew, as soon as he hit the compound, everybody would want an update. He turned to Levi. "Who's the best for IT at home?" The term *home* slipped out naturally enough.

They didn't think anything of it. But there was a tilt to the corner of Levi and Ice's lips as they smiled at each other.

"Hard to say," Ice said with a laugh. "Lots of them think they're the best. And some are definitely really good at it. But currently Stone and Harrison are working some angles. What about Tommy? Any chance he's your stalker?"

"My boobs aren't big enough. My ass is too flat, and my legs aren't long enough, and I don't have a blow-up doll personality, so I'd have to say, no."

Ice started to laugh. "Is he that bad?"

"He's eighteen, arrogant and thinks that is the epitome of the perfect woman. I don't fit the bill," she said drily. She stared down at the notepad and couldn't write one name.

Tyson nudged her. "Is there anybody in particular we should look at?"

Puzzled, she stared up at him. "I don't know. For the last six months I've been celibate, buried in my job. I have turned down even a date for coffee. I didn't notice anybody following me, looking at me strangely or being overly amorous." She put her pen down. "I have no idea."

Chapter 5

I T WAS A daunting moment for Kai to stare down at the blank page and to realize, in the last six months, she had no idea who she'd come in contact with who could be doing this.

"It could be as nebulous as the bank teller or as close as a business connection," Ice said.

"Or a past friend who may have contacted you," Tyson added. "Or somebody from the military who liked you a little too much. He could be out now. Decided to come back and see if you're interested."

"It can also be somebody who you don't know," Ice said gently. "It could be somebody who just, in their mind, said you're perfect. And he'll make this happen one way or another."

"From my research I learned stalkers can have a very strange mind-set," Tyson said. "We have to assume he's mentally unstable."

Ice took a deep breath and nodded. "You know who you need to put down here, Kai. Start with everybody you work with. If you know the neighbor across the way in your apartment building. If you know the doorman. If you know your bank teller by name. Anybody like that."

Kai reached for her phone and looked through her Contacts.

Levi said, "Don't worry about those. Everybody on that list we'll take a good look at."

She raised her gaze and studied him. "Really?"

His voice was hard when he said, "Really."

She shook her head and said, "Well, I don't have anybody else to add to this then. The men here in my Contacts will all be business acquaintances or friends. If they aren't listed here, I don't have contact with them."

"Then tell us who or what they are, what their relationship is to you."

"That I can do."

The waitress brought menus while they continued to work. Kai ordered the Caesar salad and didn't hear the rest the conversation as she tried to make sense of the long list.

She stared at one name in particular. Rob Goring. "I have no idea who this is." She glanced from one to the other. "I know a lot of people are on this list, but this one doesn't ring a bell. Neither does Ben Jones or Thomas Getty."

"Well, put them down with an asterisk beside their names. We'll start with them," Levi said.

She stared at him in surprise. "Why?"

"He had your phone long enough to put a tracker in it. It would take about ten seconds to put his name or a half-dozen names into the Contact list."

"Sure, but why bother?"

"To make it look like you were friends already, from a cop's point of view or a boyfriend's too. Or to make it look like you had a lot of men in your Contacts list. And, before you ask why again, just think of all the ugly reasons he'd do that. Including making it look like you deserve whatever is coming to you. There is logic in his actions. Just because we don't know what it is, doesn't mean it doesn't exist."

Her stomach got a sickly sense; her skin crawled at the back of her neck. She stared down at her phone and said, "I don't think I can eat lunch now."

"It's more important than ever."

She gazed at Tyson in anger. "I don't like where you're going with that."

"You've got training. You know how bad things can get."

Her breath gusted out along with some hard memories from her training and the years she'd spent in the military. His words were damn true. But leaving that world behind had been a whole lot easier than she had thought. She'd expected to feel strange and uncomfortable, but she'd thrown off that life with joy. The old Kai didn't fit the new Kai. Trying to crawl back into that skin didn't work easily.

"You're also never to be alone anymore."

"I don't trust anybody, other than you guys. But I can't impose on you for help."

"Stop," Ice said. "This isn't a job. You're our friend."

"It's not that easy. You guys will put a ton of man-hours into this in the end. Who'll reimburse you for all that?" she asked. Inside she was horrified—and her heart warmed—at their offer of help.

"I'd tell you how we take on pro bono cases all the time," Levi said, "but I know that would piss you off. On the other hand, I want you pissed off. I want you angry. I want you to look at this guy and see him for what he is. He's a creep, trying to ruin your life. Yet, you need to stay calm. You need to be in control. And you need to make sure that fear *never, ever* is in the front-row seat again."

Getting her head wrapped around this wasn't easy. Suddenly her neighbor's face popped up. "Steve Rossi. He has the apartment across from me. Henry..." She thought about it for a moment longer. "Henry Springer?" She frowned. "He was a supply clerk. He was always just kind of"—she looked over at Ice and shrugged—"creepy."

"Good. Keep going."

Accepting what she needed to do, she managed to add another half-dozen names to the list. When the waitress returned with their food, she put down her pen. "It seems stupid because these men have nothing to do with me now."

"Maybe, maybe not," Levi said, accepting the plate from the waitress. "But somebody does."

"I can set up surveillance," Tyson offered.

"What kind of surveillance?" Kai asked.

"It would be nice to see the action outside on your street."

"We checked with Detective Mannford about the city cameras, but they are only on the main traffic intersections and not on the residential side streets. Not only that, but the front of your apartment building is hidden by large trees so any city-street cameras would have a hard time capturing a clear picture. It's an older building with standard security, not one with a high-end camera system in the hallways, elevators or stairwells, so a dead end there too," Tyson said.

She stared at him. "You're ready to set up something now?"

He nodded.

She took a bite of her salad. "We could set up a camera inside my vehicle. That might show if somebody is near it and gets inside. The chances are they'd have a key already made."

"When you take it home, park it and leave it there."

She raised an eyebrow. "I still have to get to work and

have a lot of things to do around town."

He nodded. "We brought in two vehicles. One has been loaded with sensors to pick up other electronics. So you can drive that for the next week or so, and we'll see if somebody tries to penetrate the vehicle or track you again."

"This is hardly fair," she protested. "You guys are taking on way too much." She looked around but only saw hard faces. She shrugged. "Okay, but keep track of what you spend," she said. "I'll see what I can pay back over time."

"We'd rather take it out of our pocketbook than out of your hide," Ice said.

Kai realized just how good a friend this group had ended up being. She glanced at Tyson to see his hard dark eyes locked on hers. When he gave a clipped nod, she realized he included himself in that group. And she smiled this time, a warm welcoming smile and said, "Thank you."

TYSON DIDN'T LIKE anything about this. They had to find this guy. And fast. "You need to be with somebody at all times," Tyson said. "It can't be somebody from work just because you feel like nobody at work would do this. One of them could be your stalker. We need a full list of who works for you and what their role is."

He waited for her to glare at him. He understood the money issue involved in her mind. But, if Levi said anything about the expense, Tyson would sign up and do it for free himself. He didn't need to think how Tracy would feel about it. He knew she would be on his case, urging him to protect Kai. Just because she had to leave this life early didn't mean Kai should leave the planet early too because of negligence. He glanced at Levi and said, "I know you were sending me out on a job. If you have somebody else who can go, I'll stay with Kai for free."

Levi's eyes narrowed ever-so-slightly as his brain kicked in. Kai's gasp and immediate refusal was shut down by Ice's hard stare. *Good.*

Tyson didn't drop his gaze from Levi. Tyson wanted to keep his job, but he had to keep Kai safe. He didn't know how much Levi knew about their history, but then Levi gave him a nod.

"Agreed. We'll discuss the money factor later."

Kai protested. "Hell no, Tyson. You have a job to do. Go and do it."

He turned and drawled, "I intend to. You're now my job."

She snorted and sat back. "That's not what I meant."

"Too bad. You got into a situation, and now we'll help you get out."

"I'll be fine," she said adamantly.

"And how do you think Tracy would feel if I let her best friend get hurt when I could've stepped in and done something about it?"

She opened her mouth to blast him, but the words didn't come out. In a low voice she said, "That's not playing fair."

"I'll play any way I have to if it keeps you safe." He almost smiled at the glare on her face. She looked like a child who had just been schooled unfairly. She didn't like the situation she was in, and there was no way to know how cooperative or uncooperative she would be. But he wouldn't let her stay unprotected, particularly as Levi had given his stamp of approval. He turned to Levi and said, "Thank you."

Levi shrugged. "Somebody has to stick to her like glue.

Obviously you two have a history, so maybe this is a good time to work it out. We need you, Kai, to come back and forth with your new toys. I don't really want any bad blood between the two of you either."

"Won't happen," Tyson said quietly. "Kai and Tracy were best friends. Our shared history is just the person we lost in common."

"I gathered that." Levi picked up the massive burger on his plate and started eating.

Tyson realized how good it looked, wondering at his sudden appetite, and picked up his burger and dug into it. He noticed Kai played with her salad. She might be uncomfortable with him as her bodyguard, but she'd get over it.

Or not.

Her choice.

He wasn't going anywhere.

Chapter 6

AFTER LUNCH KAI said, "At least let me pick up lunch. Then I have to go back to the office."

"Why?" Tyson asked. "No one is there."

She laughed. "No. But I have work to do and could get something done because I won't be bogged down by a million interruptions."

He gave her a long, slow thoughtful look and then nodded. "First we'll get you a burner phone while we're here at the mall. Second, we'll drop off your vehicle at your apartment."

"That'll break routine. Normally I'd go to work. So we should drive back to work and then at the end of my workday, drive home again."

Levi stepped into the conversation. "Try to stick to as normal a routine as possible. We don't want to tip off the stalker that we're on to him."

"I *wish* we were on to him. I have no problem hitting enemies. But I need to see them in order to hit them." She paid for lunch as the others milled around behind her. Outside Tyson stepped in front of her. She tried to go around him and then realized he had blocked her deliberately. Behind his back she muttered, "He's not a sniper."

"How do you know?" he asked calmly.

She froze. After a moment she let out her breath. "You're

right. I don't know. I'm trying to just ignore this, make light of it and hope it goes away."

"And it might. Maybe that's better. But I hate to think he'll go underground and do this to somebody else."

"Or come back in a year or two when you're alone," Ice added.

Under her breath she muttered, "Shit." She turned to Levi and Ice and gave both hugs. "We'll see you in a couple days." She tried to dart around the immovable block in front of her, only to find herself once again stopped.

He held out his arm and said, "It wouldn't hurt him to find out you have a love interest."

"*Love interest*? Is that even a current phrase?"

"Tracy always said I was a bit of a dinosaur."

Kai winced. "She wouldn't have meant it in a bad way."

He turned. "No, she didn't. But it doesn't change the fact that I am who and what I am."

At her vehicle, he walked to the driver side and opened the door for her. She remembered his manners were always first and foremost. He looked after the ladies, particularly the one he was with. She waited until he walked around to the passenger side and got in beside her. She remembered all the conversations where Tracy had gushed over this man. At the time Kai hadn't appreciated the gushing. She'd wanted him herself. But it had been obvious he'd had eyes for Tracy only. And now with Tracy gone, Kai could consider a relationship with Tyson, but she didn't think Tyson was ready. And he might never be ready to have one with her. Would he always see Tracy when he looked at Kai?

Tracy's last words haunted Kai once again. How could she take care of this man when he wouldn't even acknowledge a relationship other than being her bodyguard?

The tables were turned; she couldn't take care of him, but he was bound and determined to take care of her. And that was bad news for him. That SEAL sense of honor, that duty to serve and protect was really strong in them. Most of the military had it to some extent, but all SEALs she'd met really had it.

On Tyson's orders, she drove first to pick up a simple cell phone, then drove them back to the office, her mind filled with all the things she needed to do. When she pulled into the parking lot, she raised an eyebrow at the vehicles. "Apparently the office *isn't* empty."

"Are you expecting the staff to come back?"

"Not after talking to Tommy."

She got out, locked the vehicle and led him to the side door. Using her keys, she unlocked the building's outside door and held it open for him. But he stood in the parking lot, studying the layout of the vehicles. It was almost as if she could see the computer in his brain cataloguing what was there, who was there. She wouldn't be at all surprised if he was memorizing the license plates. When he finally turned toward her, he studied the entrance door and the security system.

She motioned inside and said, "Are you ready?"

He stepped in and waited until she came up behind him, went around him to lead the way forward. She went up a simple landing of several steps, turned to make sure he was following her, only to find he was testing the door behind her. She knew she should be thankful, but she'd never once questioned whether the door locked behind her or not. As the door closed, the security system engaged the red light above. He studied it for a long moment, then turned and followed her up the stairs.

She wondered what it took to have a mind like that. Tracy always said he was almost pedantic in his thinking. Very solid, very analytical, very thorough. Kai just hadn't had a chance to see it up close and personal, like right now.

Inside the building on the second floor, she pointed out their offices and said, "We're at the far end."

He never said a word, just followed behind her. She tested the door to the office, but it was locked. That was also bizarre. She used her keys and unlocked it. Opening up, she stepped inside and froze. Nobody was here. With her hands on her hips, she stood inside the entrance and studied the layout.

Behind her, Tyson asked, "Problems?"

"The vehicles are in the parking lot, but the office is empty."

"Meeting?"

"Must be because the door was locked."

She walked through the hall to their meeting room to find it open. Her four employees were there with her partner, Warren. Just as she approached, she heard him say, "We have to take into account that somebody might have hacked not only her phone and her email but her access here. We need to lock her out of everything."

Anger flashed through her. She stepped into the room. "I wouldn't do that if I were you."

Everybody turned to look at her. And guilt crossed many of their faces.

She leaned against the doorjamb, crossed her arms and studied their faces. "Interesting expressions. What are you up to, Warren?"

"Nothing. But we have to keep our business safe."

"By locking out one of the owners?" Her voice was deadly soft.

Tommy winced. "We wouldn't have locked you out completely." Then his gaze widened as he looked past her shoulder. He glanced over at one of the other men, Larry, a good friend of Tommy's but not quite as brilliant, and then back at her. Nathan and Jerome were also friends but not as close to Tommy as Larry was.

"I didn't know we had a visitor," Warren said brightly, then glanced from Kai to the man behind her.

She knew Tyson would be there. Large, capable, his face almost cold, he was responsible for the shift in the men's energy. Nothing like a group of geeks who wanted to be men suddenly realizing when a real one was in the room.

All the geeks calmed down, but Warren became blustery. He came over with a hand out and said, "Hi, I'm Warren. This is my company."

Tyson ignored the man.

Warren withdrew his hand and backed up a few steps.

"No," Kai said, "this is *our* company. And if I ever hear talk of locking me out of access to my own company again, then we're talking lawsuits," she said in a hard tone. "As of right now you're on notice." She pulled out her phone, speed-dialed her lawyer and explained Warren's actions.

"I'll take care of it."

She pocketed her phone and stared at her slimy partner.

Warren sat down in his chair with a thud.

Instantly, the rest the group's attention snapped. Tommy said, "Hey, hey. No need to panic. We don't want that kind of trouble just because he was worried."

"You attended a private meeting, excluding me, and you discussed locking me out of my own company …" she said, making each word extremely clear. "Where in all of that do you see a good working relationship?"

The four employees looked at each other. Larry said, "Hey, we're sorry. That's not our intention." But something was off in his tone. Not quite a sneer but a long way from easing her irritation.

She snorted. "Maybe not but, from where I stand, I don't see anything that gives me confidence in your words or your actions."

Warren's nose was in the air when he said, "Don't get your panties in a twist. That's the problem with bringing a woman on board."

She'd have said something, but she'd heard this line way too many times. She did feel Tyson stiffen behind her. And she knew he didn't understand. He had never talked down to a woman in his life. Tracy wouldn't have allowed it. Ice certainly would not allow it. And Kai doubted anybody else in his world would've.

She looked at Warren with disgust. "Keep your macho male insecurities in check. You and I are about to have a very open, face-to-face talk over what you just tried to arrange."

He gave her a snake-oil-salesman smile. "I have your best interests at heart. But the company is not going down because you've been lax."

Tyson said, "How has she been lax?"

If she hadn't been watching Warren's face, she would've missed it. But he winced and backed up slightly in his chair.

She snorted. "I haven't been lax at all."

Warren held up his hand. "Nothing personal, stranger, but I don't know who you are. For all I know, you're her lawyer too, and I'm not saying anything without my lawyer present."

She could feel the four staff listening anxiously. If something was going on with the company, there was a good chance the staff jobs were about to go up in smoke. She could see the employees would listen to Warren, though maybe not understand the extent of what was going on. Like she hadn't either. Up until now.

"I hadn't realized you would try to get rid of me. That of course does change things." She gave him a thin smile. "Especially in light of the stalker issue. I'll be sure to hand your name to the cops first."

Fortunately she had been watching his eyes when she said that. And the astonishment in his gaze was so natural she knew he couldn't be the stalker.

Warren threw his hands into the air and said, "What? Hey, no, I'm not doing anything like that."

"Just taking advantage of an uncertain situation?" Tyson asked.

Warren glared at him. "This has got nothing to do with you. I don't know who the hell you are."

Tyson introduced himself, his arms still crossed.

"And what role do you play here?" Warren asked with a sneer. "Just because she brought you into the office doesn't mean you should be privy to any of our secrets. Typical female."

Kai couldn't believe what was coming out of Warren's mouth. Nothing he'd said was what she expected him to say. She understood he was a weasel. But she'd never seen him directly attack in this way. She didn't like what she was seeing or hearing. And that meant a lot as she adored this company and the direction it was going. That Warren had set up this meeting to get somebody to shut down her access and was talking to Tyson like this was completely unacceptable.

She gave him a steely glare. "You're digging yourself into a deep hole."

"Oh, excuse me. Just because you bought into the company doesn't mean it's yours."

"It's not yours. Remember, I hold fifty-one percent of the business."

The men jumped to their feet. "What does she mean that she owns fifty-one percent? You said she only owns thirty percent."

She stared at her employees. "Sounds like he's passing on some bullshit. I bought in, plus inherited Mark's shares." Kai was distracted with Tyson's immediate focus on her at that news. Then he pulled out his phone. He needed Ice to look into Mark's death. And to look into Warren and everyone else involved in the company.

Kai shook her head, turning to set her staff straight. "It's *my* backers who came in to invest. So, if and when I go, all that goes with me. Keep that in mind the next time you have private meetings."

She turned on her heels and walked toward her office. "Tommy, have you touched any of my access passes and my sign-ins?"

"No," he said, rushing over to her. In a low voice he asked, "What did you mean, *all the backers go?*"

"They're here because of me. When I explain what's just happened, who do you think they'll follow?"

He ran his hand through his hair nervously. "Jesus, this is all I ever wanted to do."

"Then you better watch your Ps and Qs, and stop taking sides, or you'll be out of a job."

He sat down in his chair heavily. "Man, this sucks." Then he leaned over and said, "Kai, what is your guy doing?"

Startled, she turned to look and realized Tyson was no longer standing beside Warren. Instead, he was doing a complete walk around the office. "Checking it out."

"Why?"

"Because there is a stalker in my midst," she said impatiently. "I get this is all a big joke to you guys, and others want to use it to their advantage, but some asshole is out there stalking me, and that's really not something I feel like joking around about."

"So he's a security guy?"

She turned to look at Tommy, hearing the note in his voice. Of course, for anybody like Tommy who spent his life in the geek world, Tyson was all male. It was that powerful silence that said he could handle life no matter what was thrown at him. Tommy couldn't handle a relationship, and, in any situation, he was lost. She could see how Tyson would become some kind of role model for him. And that was a bit of a joke too.

"Something like that," she said drily. "And so much more."

"Did you hire him?"

"No, he's an old friend."

Tommy gave her a big grin. "*Friend.*"

She rolled her eyes, trying to remember the eighteen-year-old's lack of maturity and said, "Yes, a friend."

"OLD FRIENDS?" TYSON muttered under his breath. As descriptions went, it wasn't bad. He had very mixed feelings when it came to Kai. He'd certainly been attracted to her way back when, but there had been something about Tracy that had pulled at his heart in a way he hadn't been able to ignore.

Before Tracy's death, Kai had always been in the background. Solid, dependable and such a damn good friend to Tracy. Kai had been part of the family and yet not. It was hard to believe he had been married to Tracy less than a year. A year of his life in which he'd married, lost a child and lost his wife. He called it the year of hell.

That it had all happened within a calendar year made it that much harder. He had met Tracy at a New Year's Eve party. He'd fallen immediately. Only Tracy was gone now. And Kai was still here.

An incredibly attractive Kai ...

He returned to study the office windows. It would be hard for anybody to get in or out of this office building, short of coming through the main doors. But he'd seen way too much military action to ignore the fact that people were bound and determined to do what they wanted to do, when they wanted to do it. And, with the right skill set, the right person could do damn near anything he wanted.

As he walked toward her, he said, "How many floors in this building? Four?"

She nodded. "Yes."

"Do you have access to the roof?"

She frowned at him, her gaze going to the windows and then back to him. "I don't know, but we can take a look."

He glanced around. "I'll look. You keep your cell phone with you."

He held out a hand, and she stared at it for a moment. "What is it you want?"

"Your keys. I want to lock up from the outside as I leave."

She winced, reached into her purse and pulled out the

keys, giving them to him. As he walked toward the entrance, she knew she would get hit with questions from her staff.

Tommy turned to her. "Did he just lock us in?"

She glanced at him and raised an eyebrow. "Funny, it was locked when I arrived."

He stared at her in surprise. "Really?"

"Really."

TYSON SMILED AS he heard the conversation through his earpiece. The other piece was attached to Kai's shirt. He hadn't told her about it when he had placed it there. He'd planned to, but then they found out the office was locked, and things had gone downhill from there. He could hear in real time and was also connected to a recording unit he'd left in the office with his jacket. No way in hell they would take any chances with her life.

He quickly scoped out the stairwell and the elevator. Standard office issue, nothing surprising in any of it. The elevator could use a little maintenance. It squeaked, and he hated to hear that. He checked out the rooftop exit door and found no warning signs or alarms. Outside was a hot summer day, and the heat pounded on the roof. It was too bad people didn't make better use of the space up here. It could be an easy garden rooftop deck, a place for the office building people to come to. But it was all about making money, leasing to people who would pay on time. It had nothing to do with making the workers' lives as comfortable as possible.

He did a full scope of the building, stood approximately above her desk and looked over the edge. There was no sign of anybody being here recently. And there was no sign anybody was even contemplating approaching from this position.

But he'd be derelict in his duties if he didn't check it out. Other office buildings were close by. Some higher up. And he imagined at least one had a bird's eye view of her office. That was a concern. He took several aerial views, making sure he took them from all sides of the building. He sent those to Ice for further diagnostics. He walked back downstairs and headed for the office.

The elevator doors closed just as he approached. Instinct prodded him to head into the stairwell and go down. He didn't trust Warren one bit. Anytime money was involved, people did strange things. On the second floor, he burst through the stairwell just as the side door opened to the outdoor parking area. He could see the elevator door closing as he passed it.

He watched as Warren headed to his vehicle. As he walked past, he was talking angrily into his phone. Tyson watched as he got into a sports car, turned on the engine and drove off. Tyson memorized the license plate, then headed back up to Kai's office while he keyed in the plate number for Ice to trace too.

As he walked in, he saw the four staff members clustered around her. He listened as the men asked questions, obviously looking for reassurances.

"Look. I can't tell you much more. Obviously Warren and I are going to talk, and it'll involve lawyers. Are your jobs safe? I can't tell you that," she said simply. "So let's just leave all the negative thinking until we can settle our differences."

"Easy for you to say," Tommy said. "You have money."

"No, I don't. I put it into this company, remember?"

That had them all sitting back.

"I work, just like you. Long, hard days. I worked in the military for years and didn't get paid very much there either, and the only money I had to put in here was the inheritance my grandparents left me, even after all my years of hard labor." She stood, dropped stacks of files on the table and said, "So how about we make sure this company's successful in order to not have it go down the pipes, and I lose everything and you lose your jobs?"

Tyson leaned against one of the walls as he studied the four employees. Tommy, he'd figured out; the other three he wanted names for. He wasn't getting any vibes off them. But that didn't mean much. They were all close enough to do whatever they needed to do. They were all smart enough in the IT world to do exactly what had already been done in Kai's stalker case.

Kai glanced up, saw him and smiled. He hated that instinctively his heart warmed and his stomach melted. She'd always been special. Tracy had tortured him with all Kai's virtues day after day. Finally he told her, laughingly, that he liked Kai well enough, for Tracy to stop trying to sell Kai to him, or he might take her over Tracy. At that Tracy had shut up. And he realized what a mistake he had made a day or two later when she had asked him if he'd been serious. He shook his head at the memory.

As he approached, Kai asked, "You're shaking your head. What's wrong?"

He gave her a crooked smile and said, "Memories."

The smile fell away, and she nodded. "They hit at the wrong time, don't they?"

"For a long time, they hit every moment of the day, not just the wrong ones, so this is much easier."

"I'm glad to hear that," she said warmly. "It's been a tough couple years."

He motioned to the men around him. "I need their names."

She winced. "Yeah, I know. I'd love Warren to be the stalker, but I doubt it."

"Not likely. He likes shiny toys. In his mind you could be tarnished."

That brought a laugh out of her. But she nodded. "It's an interesting take, but unfortunately I think you're right."

"Unfortunately."

Chapter 7

KAI SAT DOWN in the chair and worked her way through a stack of paperwork and emails. Beside her Tyson worked on his phone. She didn't particularly like working on a small screen herself. She used a tablet for a lot of her work when she was not at her desk.

Finally she glanced at her watch and said, "It's four-thirty. You ready to leave?"

"Anytime you are."

She stood and shut down the rest of the computer monitors. "Okay, guys, we're heading out," she yelled out her office door to her employees in the nearby bullpen.

"We are too," Tommy said.

She glanced up to see the others standing. Waiting. Tommy gave a small shrug and said, "We felt kind of foolish when we realized somebody is really after you. If Tyson is here to watch over you, well, we should've been doing it all along."

She gave the fresh-faced kid a big smile and said, "Thank you."

"We can't have a second boss dying on us," Jerome said. "That would leave us with only Warren." He gave a mock shudder.

At that she laughed. "That wouldn't be so bad. He's just not a people person."

Nathan, the fourth member of the group, said, "Not real sure he's either. And how come he needed you to come on board?"

"Good point. I came on board because he was broke. Mark was a good friend of mine. The company was already in the first stages of bankruptcy," she said calmly. "But I highly doubt Warren let you guys know that."

"We didn't know." They stared at her in shock and looked at each other.

"Mark was a friend for a long time. He'd suggested the investment to me, knowing where I was in life and knowing my background. I was a weapons instructor in the military, as you know. We've spoken about it before. But because of that experience, I was always looking for ways to improve my methods. Mark and I discussed it, and I approached them with a deal. I knew Mark was in favor before I talked to Warren, and happily Warren was on board too. Then Mark passed away. Now possibly Warren is thinking it's a bad deal. And he might just want to change the situation."

"That's not cool."

She shrugged. "It's business." She opened the door and let everybody out. While they waited, she locked up tight. "Okay, hopefully we're good until morning."

"You don't keep anything vital on the premises do you? Tommy has it all secured and locked away, right?" Tyson asked.

"Yes, he does. We have not only backup but we have the cloud service off-site. We can't take the chance of this type of R&D work being stolen."

Tyson nodded. "I hear you there."

Outside he walked to her car, leaned against the hood and said, "Pretend you're talking to me. I want all the vehicles to leave first so we're the last ones."

She nodded in surprise. "Fine, but then can we at least talk about dinner? I know I ate lunch, but I'm not sure I enjoyed it. And I don't remember eating much of it. My stomach thinks it's empty."

He grinned. "I know a seafood place here. They have a franchise in California. Would that be up your alley?"

"Codfather's?" Her face lit up. "I love that place."

He laughed. "I think Tracy introduced me to it. We went to the California one all the time."

"I'm the one who introduced her to that restaurant."

His face changed, and his gaze swept the empty parking lot. "Okay, that's the last vehicle. Do other offices in the building stay open late?"

She shrugged. "I have no idea about the other businesses."

"Have you considered moving the business? You need more R&D space."

"I know. I'm not sure we have the funds for it."

"Right." He studied the layout of the building, took some more pictures and said, "I want to keep watch."

"You think we are being followed?" She unlocked the doors and slid into the driver's seat.

"I think your new boyfriend already knows you have a man in your life. His next concern will be how involved I am."

She gave him a startled look as she pulled from the parking lot. "You think he already knows you're here beside me?"

"Without a doubt."

TYSON COUNTED ON the stalker knowing about Tyson's

presence. What he didn't know was what the asshole wanted from Kai. There was a lot of research on stalkers, but that didn't mean everyone followed the same pattern. In truth, most were under the impression that, for whatever reason, this woman was meant to be with them. And they often believed she knew it, but for some reason was either playing hard to get or rejecting him. Both scenarios were bad news for the victim.

If this was a vengeance type stalker, that was an entirely different story. Those he could handle. Those were just pissed-off, angry men who would sooner shoot her in the parking lot than use psychological torture. He could be wrong though, and he couldn't afford to be wrong. He certainly wasn't a psychologist who specialized in stalkers.

"Any idea if you've had an intruder in your apartment?"

She gave him a startled look. "No. I don't think so."

"Would you know if someone went through it?"

She drove onto the main road thinking about it.

He appreciated that. The last thing he wanted was for her to dismiss his questions as not being relevant.

"No, I wouldn't know. I'm busy, and I don't have any special security on my door. I certainly haven't set traps to see if somebody's broken in. I'm not home very much, and, when I do come in, I'm so tired that generally I just have a shower and crash. I haven't cooked a meal in my own kitchen in months, and, even then, it was a case of eat fast and leave."

"Anything missing?"

She frowned but again didn't toss off his question as being wasted time. "I haven't had the time to really take a look."

"So will we do that before our meal or after?"

She glanced at her watch, checked where they were in terms of traffic and said, "We'll do a check first. It's closer. But afterward we'll eat. Now that you brought up Codfather's, I want seafood fettuccine with a bowl of clam chowder."

As she drove, she kept a wary eye to see if anybody was watching. The change in direction may have confused the stalker. But maybe not. She pulled into the parking lot and parked. "What about the vehicle?"

He smiled and pointed to the vehicle in the parking spot beside hers. "Yours will stay here. We're taking that one on the way out."

"Nice. I didn't know that was yours."

"It's a company vehicle," Tyson said. "Besides, we can't afford not to have vehicles in prime operating condition when we need them."

"Just like in the military?"

He snorted. "With the military, we had rigs with mechanics overhauling them." He shook his head. "They were constantly in and out of the shop. But then we ran them into the ground out of necessity."

"I understand that. Everyone at Levi's company all come from the same background and history as you. I don't imagine he runs the place quite as tight as when you were in the military, but I imagine he's always ready for the next job."

"He is," Tyson said. "As far as I can tell. But I haven't been there long enough to know. I came because Michael told me to get my ass down here. He's kept an eye on me for the last couple years and knew it was time to move in a new direction. Michael is a good judge of character, and I trust his judgment. Besides I knew Levi somewhat, and he's a good man."

She chuckled. "Michael's anything but fancy. That man is hard inside and out."

"Not true. Mercy's made a huge difference in his life. We all react differently to pain, betrayal and disillusionment. In Michael's case, he just took it a little bit harder than many. But any time a call for help went out, he was one of the first to answer."

"I think you all would, depending on the circumstances."

He kept watch as they walked to the elevator, glanced inside and stepped out. "There's nothing wrong with this but I prefer the stairs."

"Sure. I need the exercise anyway."

He glanced over at her. "I doubt that. You appear to be in pretty fine shape."

"Ice almost beat me," Kai said with a big grin. "I was damn glad we stopped when we did. I'm also pretty sure she went easy on me."

"Some competition is healthy. A lot, on the other hand, is not."

No graffiti was in the stairwell. Also no carpet. The building seemed to be stuck in the mid-80s. It had an old, sad look, but it was still respectable. She could've done worse. He presumed investing in the company had stopped her from getting a better place. On the other hand, she would have been used to living on a base. Maybe this was a step up for her. "Do you like living here?"

As they walked down the hall, she thought about her answer. "It's fine. I'm too busy to care most of the time, but I hadn't expected such a big adjustment to private life. Still, I don't really give a damn about my surroundings as long as it's functional."

"*Functional* doesn't mean much in terms of comforts."

"No." She unlocked the door, pushed it open and stepped inside.

He walked in and stopped. He raised his head and just took in the impersonal atmosphere to her apartment. As if she hadn't fully moved in. This place said so much about Kai herself. He understood how bare a military lifestyle sometimes was. But most had families to go home to after being deployed. In Kai's case, she didn't have that. And, once Tracy was gone, she hadn't had that friend base either.

"I didn't know how to fully own the space," Kai said. "So I didn't bother trying."

She'd been so busy with the company, with adjusting to life, that her apartment must not have come into the equation in any other way than a room to lay her head down. Then that's what she was used to. And staying busy would have helped her get over losing Tracy. The two had been like sisters. She'd always lit up when she was around her best friend. The two always tried to outdo the other with bigger, wilder antics. And then all that stopped with Tracy's death. Losing her best friend had changed Kai. She was no longer so daring, outrageous in her actions or so unrestrained. He'd certainly changed, so he couldn't imagine it had been any less for her either.

He did his usual walk through the apartment, checking every closet, door, under the bed and windows as she traipsed behind him and watched.

When he finally turned to her, she asked, "Does it pass your inspection?"

"Not particularly. Not if we're trying to keep you safe. There's no security, and the fire escape is eight feet from your window. You don't have any way to get down if somebody cuts off your exit. Steve Rossi lives across from you, according to what you said earlier, but the name has been removed on the directory downstairs. So chances are good that he's moved, and you didn't notice." He quirked an eyebrow at her and continued as her jaw dropped, and she turned in the direction of the front door. "That means nobody is in the apartment across from you, which means you can't call to them for help. This leaves you fairly isolated and contained." Immediately he felt bad as the color washed out of her face.

She reached up and rubbed her temple. "I forgot what you were like. Could this be much worse?"

"Absolutely." He shrugged. "You at least have a dead bolt on the front door. You do have a fire escape you could hook onto and make your way down, but that would require breaking your living room window and opening yourself up to other injuries. You have neighbors on either side who potentially could hear something if you called out. You have underground parking, which offers a small measure of security. You have both elevators and stairs, which is standard, but there's only one elevator, not two," he corrected. "In other words it's a standard apartment building with not a whole lot of security benefits."

"Right."

He studied her. "Now can you check to see if anything's missing?"

She waved her arm around the living room. "Well, I didn't have anything in here. And those boxes over in the far corner aren't unpacked because they're not really important."

"And your bedroom?"

Her face crinkled up. "I was trying to ignore that room."

She walked into her bedroom with him following a few steps behind.

His gaze landed on the unmade bed. It was hard not to imagine her small body curled up in the cozy indent from where she'd slept. It was impossible to ignore the fact the other half of the bed was flat, untouched, indicating she slept alone. He had to wonder if she wanted anybody to fill that space. He clamped down hard on his feelings, surprised they even arose.

This was Tracy's best friend. Kai wasn't for him. The fact that he was even aware of such things reminded him it was time for him to get back into relationships. It had taken all this time for him to realize he didn't want to sleep alone for the rest of his life.

As he walked to Kai's bedroom window and looked out, he understood he didn't want someone like Tracy. She'd been special. She had been a part of his life. He wanted somebody else. Maybe. He almost laughed at that. Every time he thought he was ready to step forward, doubts plagued him. He couldn't cast other woman in Tracy's mold. They wouldn't fit, and it wasn't fair to another woman. He wouldn't do that to Kai. But, when he was faced with the dynamo in front of him—her hot, tight curvy body in an intimate setting—well ... it was hard to not appreciate her for who she was.

She walked over to the closet and opened it. The interior was in direct contrast to Tracy's. Kai had almost nothing hanging except two or three dresses.

He checked the top shelf, but it was empty. He raised an eyebrow in her direction. She shrugged, pointed to the dresser.

"Pay particular attention to your lingerie."

"I was afraid you would say that." She pulled out drawers. Simple white cotton panties were nicely folded in one, and the others held camisoles, pajamas, nighties and T-shirts. Serviceable, clean, like her. None of the stuff Tracy used to love. Another difference. A good one. Kai was simplicity itself. This suited her.

After she'd gone through all the drawers, she turned to him. "I can't tell."

"Did you have anything unusual, anything special?"

She shook her head. "No." Then she frowned. "Yes. … I do. One set in a plum color …" She reached for it and froze. "It's not here."

He stepped forward. "Were both pieces together?"

She nodded. "They were tucked inside each other so, when I reached for one, I'd get both." She pulled her drawer out until it was completely off the track, laid it on the floor and searched the space behind it.

He knew what she was doing. He waited. The reality would hit her soon. "I can't find them." She started to panic and proceeded to go through every drawer. But found no sign of them. Finally she inspected the drawer's back space again and turned to look at him. "How did you know?"

"It's just one more step in the process of a stalker's mind. They are often looking for bits and pieces. Souvenirs. If it is a romantic attachment in his mind, that becomes a sexual drive. It's only natural to come looking for something of yours to take away. It's part of his trophy. He wants that piece of you close by, something he could look at, touch, feel and smell."

"I can't express how my stomach feels right now." She sank slowly onto the bed. "Because this means, not only has he been in my apartment but he's gone through my things and taken something for himself."

"Yes," Tyson confirmed. That sense of violation would never go away. She could never look at her apartment again the same way. He was sorry for that.

"What am I to do now?" She gave a broken laugh. "It never occurred to me someone would have been here. I had no idea."

"And that's the scary part." He reached out a hand, pulling her to her feet. "Let's go have dinner."

She stared at him in shock. "You expect me to eat after this?"

"I expect you to put one foot in front of the other and do what's necessary. I expect you to enjoy it. And I expect you to remember you are no longer alone."

She shook her head. "But what if he comes back?"

He pulled out his phone. "Levi's sending the team to set up video cameras."

She looked a little sick at that. "In my bedroom?"

He chuckled. "No, it does not have to be in your bedroom."

She wrapped her arms tight around her chest. "And why are we leaving if they are coming to do that?"

"So we're out of the way." He walked to the kitchen, grabbed a chair and walked to the front door. There he stepped up and installed the small camera system he'd been carrying in his pocket. When done, he stepped down and turned to look at her. "Now we can make sure no one comes inside who isn't allowed in."

Chapter 8

KAI STARED AT Tyson, dumbfounded. "You're fast."

"Now let's go so the guys can get in here." He smiled. "They'll set up some cameras in the hall, stairwell and one facing the living room to see if anybody's coming in through the fire escape."

"I never even saw the fire escape." She walked over to the living room and stared out. "The window here is solid. How could anybody possibly get in or out?"

"You're only one floor up from the street."

"Shit." It had never occurred to her when she rented this apartment that she should be looking for something safe. And now she felt like a fool.

"It's what we do. So let it go. Let's have dinner, and let the guys do their thing."

She nodded, grabbed her purse and walked out with him. She locked the door as usual and tried not to look around as they headed out. Once in the parking lot Tyson led her to a vehicle. She watched as he opened the door for her, his gaze casual and yet so aware of everything going on around them.

Then he hopped in the driver's seat, turned the key and drove out.

She let out her breath in a heavy *whoosh*. "Even in the military I didn't do this kind of stuff."

"Maybe not, but we did. So let us do what we need to do."

She settled back to relax.

If she didn't let her mind glom onto the reminder of someone invading her personal space, pawing through her underwear, she could almost deal with this. She found her appetite again. Codfather was one of her favorite restaurants when Tracy had been alive. Kai hadn't been to one since.

She walked in to find they had a reservation. As they were led to the table, she said, "When did you have time to make a reservation?"

"Ice did it."

"Okay."

They were given a window seat, overlooking the city. "It's a stunning view."

"It is indeed."

"It has a fairy-tale look," she said with a bitter note she hadn't expected to hear. "Which is so fake."

"No, it's not. Like everything else, there are layers. Just because you live in one layer doesn't mean other shadowy layers aren't below you. You just have to make sure you don't let it suck you down."

She studied the solemn man across the table from her. At first she couldn't believe Tracy and Tyson had hooked up. Maybe because she hadn't wanted them too, and they had in many ways been opposites. But, once laying eyes on each other, they'd both fallen in love. He'd been good for Tracy, toning her down, keeping her grounded. And maybe, just maybe, Tracy had lightened his life and brought joy into his world.

"What are you thinking?" he asked curiously.

She laughed. "How different you and Tracy were."

He nodded. "And it's nice we can talk about Tracy without either of us tearing up," he said with a lopsided smile. "But Tracy and I were very different. I'd like to think we were good together."

"I know she was happy. I was incredibly happy for her and you."

"But it's also because of me that she died."

Her jaw dropped. "What? Absolutely not."

"Not only was she pregnant, carrying my child," he said painfully, "but I wasn't there at the time to save her."

She realized how much this man—who went out to save the world for years—harbored his own personal sense of guilt over failing to save his wife. "The one thing you couldn't take away from Tracy was that pregnancy. She was never happier. It's what she wanted. She was desperate to have a child. The fact that everything went wrong is not your fault. Even the doctor said that they might not have saved her had she been in the hospital earlier." She watched as he forced a smile.

He motioned at the menu in front of her and said, "Take a look. They have some new items. You might want to change your choice for dinner."

She gave him the chance to change the topic. As she studied the menu, she realized they hadn't changed the menu at all but had switched it up somewhat. It wasn't hard to pick something as she had several favorites. When the waitress came around, she ordered a glass of white wine with her meal.

She probably shouldn't have the wine, but, at the same time, she knew she'd never get any sleep tonight if she couldn't relax. It didn't surprise her when he didn't order any alcohol. He drank sparingly. He'd also consider himself on the job right now.

When the meal arrived, she was grateful as the conversation lulled into something less awkward. She realized Tracy had always been part of the conversations between them. A topic that they both wanted to discuss, but neither really wanted to because of the pain. That they'd brought up her name several times now was good. Maybe they could move on.

"Are you seeing anyone right now?" she asked.

He shook his head. "Thought about it. I had coffee with a few women but haven't found anybody to go further than that with."

He raised his gaze to hers with that laser blue she'd always found so unsettling. And yet it was no longer as difficult to look at as she remembered it.

He said, "According to what you told us at lunch, you aren't either."

She shook her head. "No. The last one ended abruptly. Then I just got too busy. It will happen when it happens, but I'm not rushing into anything."

"When you say *abruptly*, what does that mean?"

She snorted. "I ended it. I walked into his place to find him in bed with another woman."

Tyson's eyebrows rose. "Understandable. Did you have an argument, or was he angry, upset?"

"Only from being caught with his girlfriend, who just laughed." She shrugged. "I tossed him his keys, turned and walked out. Haven't seen him since."

"How long were you with him?"

"Six months. We were talking about moving in together right before I found out."

He watched and filed away that information.

"His name was Wilson Warnock. I met him just after leaving the military. I probably jumped into it because he wasn't military. That was attractive at the time," she said with a laugh. "No, my heart wasn't devastated. No, he didn't seem to be angry, upset, or have any reason to come after me. We just moved on."

"Still, I'll update Ice by adding his name for her background checks. She'll let us know if she finds anything noteworthy." He quickly sent a text to Ice, then paused, watching her expression. "It's devastating to be betrayed by someone so close to us."

"Irritating, yes," she corrected. "And I was an idiot for signing up in the first place." She laughed. "It's all good."

WAS IT REALLY that simple? He couldn't imagine it being so. But then again, after Tracy, he couldn't imagine having a lighthearted or serious romance. And yet, he probably should. Dipping his toes back in the water didn't have to be taken as jumping off the deep end of the dock. But he knew that, after Tracy, he wouldn't be happy with superficial. He didn't want a lighthearted relationship. He wanted someone who would give him the high points of what he had. Compassion, commitment, loyalty and love.

His phone buzzed. He pulled it out and read the text. **Cameras have been installed**. He lifted his head and stared at her.

She frowned when she saw it. "What's the point of notifying us?"

"It will alert Ice if there's an intruder."

She stared at him and swallowed hard. He recognized that was her physical sign as she mentally paused before she blurted out whatever came to mind. Some people lost color in the face. Other people protested. But she was quiet, as if looking for control as she thought about what he said. And what he didn't say.

"Okay then." She took another bite. While she considered all this, he continued to eat. When she finished her plate, she set it off to one side, picked up her wine and settled back. "Are you staying the night?"

Heat zinged to his groin, and he slammed a lid on it. "I am." He reached across, picked the listening device off her shirt and turned it off.

She stared at it, her mouth contorting as she understood what it was. He placed it in his wallet and said, "I should've taken that off earlier. Sorry."

She stared at him in shock, glancing around. "Have they been listening into our conversation?"

"I took out my earpiece. But it's still connected. As long as we're together, we don't need it. And I don't see any reason for you and I to not remain together until your stalker is found. But, if and when we're separated, you'll have one."

His voice was hard, implacable. A few things he might bend on, but this was not one of them.

"To answer your question again, yes, I am staying the night." He added, "And every night afterward until this is done."

"You'll really put a dent in my romantic life," she complained without any heat.

He gave her a ghost of a smile and, with a devilish twinkle in his eye, said, "Or maybe I'll add some sparkle to it."

Chapter 9

HER JAW DROPPED, and, when she could, Kai said, "Are you flirting with me?"

He raised one eyebrow. "Maybe." He stared off in the distance before directing his gaze at her. "Are you against it?"

She sat back and stared. She had no idea what to think about this side of him, except to say she approved. "I'm not sure what to say," she said cautiously.

He turned that twinkle on again. "If you figure it out, let me know."

And she realized just how special a moment this really was. How much he'd jumped forward, healing with every step he took.

She didn't want to do anything to slow or halt this progress, but, at the same time, she was stunned at his playfulness, the lightheartedness that had popped out of the blue. And she struggled to adapt.

"I surprised you, didn't I?" He chuckled, the air of a little boy around him.

"What brought this on?" She leaned forward. "Not that I'm against it, mind you, but I haven't seen this fun side of you before."

"Then again you haven't played with me." Damn if that sexual innuendo didn't appear to startle him too. He laughed. "I have to admit to feeling oddly lighthearted at the moment."

"Nice to hear. You miss her," she said, which sucked as his smile fell away. She quickly added, "No, I don't mean that. It's just that I really appreciate seeing you in this happy-go-lucky mood. It's nice. You've been sad and serious for long enough."

He shrugged. "I agree. We both have been that way for long enough. I loved her, but she's gone," he said simply. "I'm ready to move on."

She beamed at him. "Good. You're too nice a person to stay sad and alone forever."

"We have a lot of history between us," he said with a teasing tone back in his voice, "but where in all of that did you think I was a nice guy?"

"I knew you were a nice guy before Tracy saw you."

He glanced at her with another raised eyebrow. "Really? Did we know each other first?"

She winced.

"I'll take that as a yes."

"It was a long time ago. And we didn't exactly know each other," she hedged.

"How long ago?"

She shrugged. "I was your neighbor."

He stared at her. "What?"

She laughed at the look of complete shock on his face. "Yes, when you lived in the apartment on Dilworth Road. The Mongolia apartments in San Diego. I was your neighbor."

He stared at her as his mouth slowly dropped open. "Seriously? I figured for sure you would say in the military ..."

At that she howled.

"I always thought I was so observant. I didn't even notice you when you were right next door to me."

"I know, right? We were neighbors for about eighteen months, then you moved out."

"Did Tracy know?"

Kai shrugged. "I never told her."

His gaze narrowed. "Why is that?"

"No reason. But no point in mentioning it." She smiled warmly. "It was obvious the two of you were right for each other."

"That's how we felt. Like it was just the two of us in the world." He stared off into the distance.

She watched him carefully. "Would it have lasted?"

He slanted her a thoughtful gaze. "I don't know. I'd like to think so. Unfortunately I'll never find out now."

"True enough."

"Did she ever give you any indication it might not last?" he asked curiously. "We had our disagreements and arguments certainly, but we didn't fight. She never said anything along those lines to me, but I know she didn't like me leaving on missions."

Kai placed her hand over his. "No, she was very happy. Tracy was a blessing to both of us. That time has come and gone, and we need to move on."

"I have moved on," he said. "I'm only just realizing how much. It was hard at the beginning. Then I turned around one day and realized I could remember her with joy, not pain." He smiled at Kai. "I hope it's the same for you."

"It is indeed." She glanced at her watch. "Are you ready to go home?"

His gaze warmed. "Absolutely." The waitress brought the bill, which Tyson paid for.

They walked to the front entrance, and Kai paused. "I

have to use the ladies' room." She turned down the hallway to the facilities. As she returned, the hall was darker. She was sure a light was on earlier.

She headed back toward the main section of the restaurant.

There was no sign of Tyson. She presumed he went to the washroom himself.

The hostess walked over with a folded note. "Your boyfriend said to give you this." She turned and walked away, saying, "Have a good night."

Surprised she opened it. Written in block caps was the word **DECIDE**.

She glanced down at the bottom of the page where two more words were. **Or else**. She carefully folded the note, turned back to the hostess, only to find her gone. Kai looked around, hoping to catch sight of her again and then had to wonder if she worked here. The woman hadn't been wearing a uniform, neither had she been carrying anything that indicated she worked here. But for some reason Kai had assumed she did. And that, of course, was the wrong thing to do.

She turned slowly but found no sign of her. She was probably just one of the patrons. However, there was still no sign of Tyson. When she circled back again, she saw him striding toward her from the men's room.

As soon as he caught sight of her face, he asked, "What happened?"

Without a word she handed over the message. "A woman I thought worked here handed this to me and said my boyfriend asked her to give it to me."

Tyson studied the note in his hand, nodded and said, "Time to go." He opened the door, held it for her and walked out in front of her. He reached behind him.

There was something about the way his hand extended toward her that she could get used to. That proprietary air said he knew she'd comply. Not with arrogance but with caring. She slid her fingers into his, and he tucked her up close.

Dusk was settling in, but it wasn't pitch black yet. He walked her to the SUV, unlocked the passenger door and stayed between her and the rest of the world as she got in. When she was inside and buckled up, he closed the door and walked around. But instead of getting in, he stood outside and made a phone call.

She knew he was calling Levi. She settled into her seat, wishing she could question the woman. Instead, Kai had let a perfect opportunity slip by. Just then the woman walked out of the restaurant with an older man. The two were holding hands. Kai unlocked the vehicle and bolted out.

"Kai, stop," Tyson yelled.

She raced up to the woman, stepped in front of her, saying, "Hi, remember me?"

The woman raised her eyebrows.

"Do you remember who gave you the note? Is that him over there?" Kai motioned toward Tyson. "He's my boyfriend. Was it him?"

The woman glanced at Tyson and frowned. "No. This guy was shorter, younger, with dark hair." She glanced at Tyson again, then back to Kai. "Not anything like him."

Kai knew exactly what she meant. The man beside her stepped up, wrapped his arm around the woman protectively and said, "Is there a problem here?"

Kai smiled at him. "I need a description of the man who gave her the note she passed to me. The note was a threat—

one of many—but so far nobody's identified who my stalker is."

"Oh, my gosh." The woman placed her fingers over her lips in shock. "That's terrible." She stared at her partner and then turned to Kai. "I just barely saw him. He stepped in front of me and said, 'Excuse me. When my girlfriend comes out, could you hand her this note?'"

"And did he walk out afterward?" Tyson joined Kai, asking the woman to go over the scenario once again with him, with a few more sharp questions.

When there were no more questions to ask, Kai took the woman's name and number and said, "Thank you for this."

Tyson nodded. "We'd appreciate it if you would meet with the police department's sketch artist. I've already texted them to expect you. Thank you for your help."

The couple hurried off.

She turned to Tyson. "Well?"

"We have a little more than we had before. It's a start. Now let's get you back home safe and sound."

"WELL, YOU WERE right," Kai said as Tyson pulled the vehicle out of the restaurant's parking lot and headed to the main road. They were about ten, maybe fifteen minutes away from her apartment.

"Right about what?"

"Right about him keeping watch on me," she groaned. "But how mad will this make him?"

"Pretty mad. Which is to be expected. Competition is not in the cards."

"So we can expect an attack from him now?"

"We're always expecting that—but, yes, we should expect an escalation in his behavior."

She sighed in frustration. "That's not helpful."

"We need to stay alert. That's both good and bad. Good in that he'll show his hand soon. Bad in that we don't know in what way. That means this ugly situation can get out of hand very quickly."

"In what way?"

"You know exactly what way. He'll likely make an attempt to get rid of me. Then he'll make you pay for it because, by not getting rid of me yourself, you're telling him how you're choosing me over him."

"Even though I don't know him? Even though he's not my lover or my partner?"

"In his mind every day he's stepping closer and closer to the two of you being the reality. That you can't see or won't accept that is not his problem. He'll believe you're either playing hard to get, cheating on him or any number of other sick possibilities. Remember that we're not talking about a normal mind here. We're talking about somebody who wants something and plans to get it regardless of the consequences."

"I don't like the idea of him going after you."

"Oh, I do like the idea of him going after me," Tyson countered. "I volunteered for this. I knew exactly what I was getting into, so don't you worry about me."

"You might be a big macho soldier," she said with spirit, "but I've certainly met more than my fair share of those. Bullets don't give a damn who you are ... They will kill anyone."

"They do indeed."

She was quiet after that.

He drove the fastest route home and parked at the

apartment spot Levi had reserved for him.

She shot him a sharp look but didn't say anything.

That was good. She was learning to follow his lead without questioning everything.

HE LED THE way, noting cameras installed at the location. Some were hidden, some open. At her apartment he stepped back and held out his hand for the key. She gave it to him. He unlocked the door and pushed it open, stepping in front of her. He waved at the camera at the top, then turned on a lamp. Instantly a warm glow filled the room. He took a quick pass through the apartment. Empty and secure.

She walked in, put her purse on the table and waited for him to be done.

He came out of the bedroom and leaned against the doorjamb. "How you feeling?"

"Fine," she said with a smile. "How can I not be? I have a big bad former SEAL here to look after me, and apparently a whole team I know in the background."

He smiled, but he could sense her disquiet. "It'll be okay," he said. "You know we won't let anybody hurt you."

She gave him a wan smile. "You won't as long as you're capable of fighting. I've seen firsthand how bullets rip into the human body, and it doesn't matter how strong or how willing the person is, they still die," she said softly. "Even with my hours of martial arts, it's the same deal."

He nodded. "Left or right?" he asked.

She stared at him in confusion, then shrugged. "Left? But I have absolutely no idea what we're talking about, so maybe right."

"Do you want the left side of the bed or the right side of

the bed?"

Her jaw dropped. "Oh, no. You don't get to sleep in my bed. It's out in the living room for you."

"Oh, no. I'll be sleeping in the bed beside you."

"Oh, hell no." She walked into her bedroom and slammed the door shut.

He laughed. It started as a low chuckle. Like a rusty unused one, and, finally unable to stop it, it rolled out freely.

She opened the door and stared at him. "I've never heard you laugh like that."

Still laughing, holding his side, he walked into the living room and collapsed on the couch. "It's been a long time." He said it with the odd chuckle still escaping.

"Glad you think it's funny." She glared at him. "You're still sleeping in the living room."

"I had planned on it," he said. More chuckles escaped. "*Your reaction.*"

She came out like the dynamo she was, and, with one of the pillows in her hand, she started beating him. She hit him on the legs and the head and stomach and just wouldn't stop. "You ... You ..."

Then he howled.

Finally the only way to get her to stop was to grab her, drag her onto the couch, and the two of them rolled off onto the floor. He quickly rolled over and pinned her down. But he forgot—just for a hair of a second—how she was damn near as good at martial arts as he was. The next thing he knew, he found himself on his back with her pinning him to the floor. He was laughing so hard that his ego didn't even mind.

"If you think you can strong-arm yourself into my bed, you've got another think coming."

He slipped his arm around her again, tucking her under him again. This time he grabbed her arms, pulled them up over her head and held tight. Slowly, ever so slowly, he pressed his pelvis against hers. She twisted against him. He couldn't tell if it was in response or if she was trying to get away.

Then he decided he better find out for sure. He lowered his head and kissed her. Not a light exploratory kiss. But an over-the-top kiss, out of touch with the subtleties, because he wanted to know exactly where he stood. *Now.* Driving deep, he searched for her response. When she flung her arms around his neck, her thighs wrapped around his hips, and kissed him back, he froze. And then he lost it in a haze of heat that burned through his restraint, burned through the years of pain, and somehow he stood in the aftermath—reborn. He stroked her face, ... caressing her cheeks, her eyes, her nose as he kissed her over and over again until he felt something else.

He lifted his head to see tears slowly tracking down her face. He froze again. "Did I hurt you?" he asked, hating himself for bringing her to this.

She reached up a finger, covered his lips. "No, don't think that."

But it was hard not to think that.

She grabbed his hair and dragged him back down where the heat of her mouth seared into him, sealing the two of them together, melting them into one.

And yet, they still had so many damn clothes between them. He groaned.

She wrenched her mouth free and said, "My room, now." She pushed him off, hopped to her feet and raced into the bedroom. Slower, but not by much, he followed the trail of clothing as she stripped in front of him, ending up on the far side of the bed in nothing but a thong. He reached for her, but she backed up a step.

"Hell no. You're wearing way too many clothes."

"I can take care of that," he said, his voice heavy with passion.

When he was down to his boxers, she stepped forward. "I'll take care of that last bit."

His body shuddered as she slipped her hands under the elastic and over his erection and slowly dropped to her knees in front of him.

He closed his eyes, his mind going blank as she laid her lips on his shaft. "Jesus," he whispered in a guttural groan.

"Keep calling. He might help you out." She gave a husky laugh, adding, "But I doubt it."

She grasped him in her hands, slowly stroking the full length of him, her fingers gently cupping the sack between his legs. All the while he stood frozen, his body trembling. It had been so damn long, and yet, at the same time, he knew he couldn't go there as a small part of him said it hadn't been long enough.

Pulling back, he picked her up in his arms and carried her to the bed.

"So impatient," she teased.

"It's been too long," he admitted. Way too damn long. He was afraid to go too fast. Of losing control. Of not giving her the satisfaction she needed because he was out of practice.

She opened her thighs wide. "Come to me now."

Her voice was dark, the color of midnight as he dropped down, covering her like a heated blanket. He grasped her hips, held her firmly in place and plunged deep inside. The cry ripped out of his throat as she wrapped around and held him tight. And then he was lost. Pounding, driving deep, the promise of foreplay long gone in this madness.

The climax ripped through him, his body arching, the sounds coming from him something he'd never heard before.

Still shuddering, he collapsed onto his elbows and stared down at her. And knew she hadn't reached her own climax. Under his breath he whispered, "Damn."

She stroked his face gently. "No. This time was for you. There's no rush. We've got all night."

He kissed the tip of her nose, his tongue sliding along her cheekbones. "What makes you think I'm good for another round?" She wiggled beneath him, and his eyes opened wide as he felt his body spring to life yet again. "That shouldn't happen," he protested.

She chuckled. "It'll happen. Again and again and again."

Chapter 10

DEEP IN THE night she shifted in the big bed. Instantly, his arms tugged her closer. Even while asleep he wanted her close.

Tears burned her eyes.

She didn't want to miss a moment in his arms, moving even closer, her body pressed to his chest, her head on his shoulder. This night was so damn special. She was scared to fall asleep, then waking up to find it would be different. That everything would change. She relaxed her head against his hot skin and closed her eyes, feeling his strength from within.

"You okay?"

She kissed him gently. "I'm fine. Just afraid the time is going by too fast, and soon this will be over."

His arms squeezed her gently. "This moment might be over, but we can create more moments."

She smiled, shifting slightly so she could look up at him. His eyes were closed, and his breath was still heavy and deep. "Promise? Promise this won't change in the morning?"

His lids opened enough that his slumber-warm eyes packed a powerful punch. She stared, mesmerized at the passion in him. "We came to this point on our own. What we make of it from here is ours to decide. Nobody else tells us what we can or cannot do. We have no reason to be sorry about this. We don't answer to anyone else, just each other. He reached out and stroked her chin, his fingers soft, gentle, moving up her cheek to brush the hair off her forehead. "If you want this moment to continue, let's make that happen."

"And do you want it to continue?"

He leaned forward and dropped a kiss on her forehead. "Absolutely."

With a happy smile she snuggled back into his arms. He shifted down slightly. She rolled onto her back as he rose up over her. "Nobody said we were done now."

And he slipped inside. On his knees he held her hips, pulled her tight, scooped her arms up over her shoulders and slowly started to move.

This wasn't the heated coupling of before. It was a slow, gentle meeting of mind and body. Skin sliding over skin. Hot gazes locked on each other. Bodies twisting and shuddering as their need rippled through them.

"So special," he murmured.

His words echoed in her mind. "I want to keep this feeling between us forever," she whispered. "I don't want to lose it."

"And there's no need to." He outstretched his hand to cup her breasts. "I have no objection to spending every waking moment like this," he said with a wicked grin.

She smiled and propped herself up on her elbows, her back arching in delight. "So damn good."

Her words spurred him on until she was forced to hook her arms around his neck and hold on for the ride.

When she woke a second time, she was still curled up in his arms. She smiled. She didn't want him to rush into anything. This was too important. She wanted a long time, not just a fun time. She closed her eyes and tried to sleep again.

But as she lay here, she was filled with a sense of disquiet. She frowned, lifted her head off the pillow.

Tyson's arms tightened around her shoulders, his voice low against her ear as he whispered, "Stay still."

Wide awake, she turned to meet his gaze as he listened intently. She couldn't hear anything else, but she would trust his instincts any day.

When he slowly slipped from the bed and pulled on his jeans, taking a handgun from his holster, she realized this was a whole lot more than nothing. She had to get one of her own and fast. She didn't want to be left behind in bed so she quickly dressed. He held up his hand and motioned for her to tuck up against the closet. Flat against the wall he sidled up to the bedroom door and pressed his ear to it. How could he hear anything? Maybe he didn't as he made no motion to open the door.

Frowning, he stayed in that position. Then he shook his head and shrugged. He opened the door and stepped out.

She wanted to call him back. Did he know if the intruder had left?

Then the tension in his shoulders eased.

She didn't get it. She was still too keyed up inside. She followed him from the room. Several steps behind, she watched and waited. But she couldn't see anything. When he walked in a straight line to the living room window, she realized he'd seen something. She raced to his side, and he pointed out a note stuck on the outside of the window, close to where the slider opened. The writing was visible.

She bent down and read it.

I know what you're doing.

She gasped and spun to look at Tyson. "What does that

mean? Does he know we're hunting him down? How could he possibly know that?"

Tyson's face grim, he said, "He either heard or saw something he shouldn't have. Or ... he assumes we're tracking him because he knows you've gone to the police. Again, we can't know anything for sure." He took a photo of the note and sent it to Ice. Then he hit a speed-dial number, and she listened as he talked to Levi.

"Any chance we had cameras on the roof? Or outside?" Tyson leaned his head toward the window as if looking at the roof, then his gaze cut toward her. He nodded. "Right. Check the feeds. Send me any faces you can capture that you can't discount, and I'll ask her about them." Their conversation went on a little longer.

As she curled up in the corner of the couch, she realized it was already five in the morning, and her day had already started. She didn't know where she would go from here, but the asshole obviously knew they were watching him. It also meant he had skills. Mad skills. And that completely changed everything. Who the hell did she know who could do something like this?

Tyson stood in front of her. "Ice is checking all the feeds to see if they can catch sight of him. He could've done this in a couple ways. One was coming down the roof. One was climbing up the fire escape, which wouldn't have been all that hard." He took a deep breath. "Even possibly shooting the message from a paintball gun. They are easy enough to adapt to shooting all kinds of missiles. Most aren't terribly powerful, but they are definitely good enough to do this."

She shot him a startled look, worked her way through the information and then nodded. "Still, it's pretty ballsy. And not very stalkerlike. This seems like a different skill set."

She groaned. "So now what do we do?"

"You won't like this part," he said quietly. "We wait. Everybody is searching feeds, checking out names, going through your history."

At that she straightened her back. "My history?"

"Yes, your history. He has intersected your life somewhere. Unfortunately it could be as simple as someone at your bank, at a friend's party, or it could be something else. But we will find him."

WAITING WAS NOT anything anybody wanted to do. Particularly him. He'd take action over inaction any day. From the defeated look on her face he realized, of course, she would too. He sat on the couch beside her, pulled her into his arms. "Can you sleep again, even though the night's almost over?"

She laughed. "And how much sleep did I get after we turned out the lights?"

He grinned and dropped a kiss on her temple. "How about a run then?"

She turned and gave him a startled look, then frowned. "It depends how far you're running these days."

He chuckled. "Why don't we do three miles, and see how you do without any sleep? Neither one of us will have much energy left. But I'm too keyed up to not have an outlet."

She grinned. "Wouldn't you rather go to the gym and have me kick your butt?"

"You probably could do that anywhere—no need for a gym—but, if you'd rather that over a run, I'm up for it."

She shook her head. "I don't want to be inside. I would

rather be outside with the wind in my hair and on my face. I hadn't realized just how much I miss being outdoors. My job here entails me traveling from my apartment to my vehicle, my vehicle to my office and back again. If I get out in the field, I'm a happy camper. But it's still not enough."

"We'll have to get you out more."

"With all this going on, do you think it's safe?"

He nodded. "I'll be hooked up in the communication system, so they can hear us as we run."

She nodded and scrambled off his lap. "Then I'll get changed and have a shower when we come back."

He watched as she disappeared. She seemed okay, unnerved a little bit, but that was another reason for going for a run. The exercise would be good for them both. He'd love to take care of the issue in another way, and, if it hadn't been for this disturbance, the lovemaking would've ensued again, but that mood was gone. This was a better option for the moment. He glanced down at his jeans and T-shirt and realized they were hardly the best jogging choices, but at least he had his running shoes, and they were only doing three miles.

He got up and grabbed a couple water thermoses from her cupboard and filled them. By the time he turned around, she was in front of him, wearing leggings and a sports bra with a tank top. She pulled a pair of running shoes from the entryway closet, squatted down and tied them up. Then she bounced to her feet and did a couple stretches. She turned, gazed at him and said, "You ready to go?"

He nodded. "Absolutely."

She gave him a look and said, "You're not exactly dressed for a run."

"I'll be fine."

She nodded and unlocked the door. Once outside on the street, she asked, "Which way?"

"No matter which way, we're looking at a cement jungle. So pick your favorite route."

"I haven't got one. So any route will do."

"I prefer back routes then." He started to run at a slow jog to warm up. He took the first right, staying in the back corners. "My watch can give us distance."

"Do you have one of those mileage apps on it? I had it on my old phone."

"I do."

For the first little bit they ran in silence. Shaking their arms, kicking their legs, and pushing off the unsettling start to their day. But they quickly settled into a rhythm.

She pointed out a park, saying, "It's got a good set of fields in the back."

They headed in that direction as he kept a watchful eye around them. He let her run ever-so-slightly ahead and matched his strides to hers. She might have dropped running on a regular basis, but she was no slouch when it came to fitness. He knew perfectly well she could probably outrun him. In many ways they were equally matched. And after last night, he realized they were a whole lot better matched than he had any right to expect. He was still stunned by the speed with which they'd come together and the absolute sense of rightness through it all. Worry still nagged at him, but he wanted to believe Tracy would be happy for him. It'd been two years. Surely that was long enough.

"I need to adjust my shoelace when we get to the park," Kai said, her breath slow and steady. "The left one's too tight."

"We can stop now if you want."

She shook her head. "No, I'm good."

They crossed the street, enjoying the absence of traffic, and at the park they slowed to a walk. She pulled up to a bench, lifted her foot onto the seat and untied her shoe. She readjusted it, bounced in place a few times and turned with a smile. "Race you to the end of the field." And just like that she jackrabbited to the left.

Unprepared for her move, he was given an instant handicap. "Hey," he protested, racing behind her. "That's cheating."

Her laughter trilled behind her as she picked up speed. She was one of the few people who could just churn up energy. She was damn good at it, almost like watching a bullet fly forward. It was all he could do to keep up with her. But no way in hell would he let her beat him too badly.

With his lungs pumping, his feet pounding, he surged behind her, caught up to her and was almost ready to overtake her when she had another burst of speed and bolted past him again. He was a good ten steps behind when she hit the end of the park, bounced into the fence and turned to laugh at him. He made no attempt to slow his speed but bounced into the fence over her.

He braced himself just before he came up against her. With their bodies pressed tight together, he lowered his head and kissed her. Hot, sweaty and ravenous, he devoured her mouth with the heat he thought would be long spent. She wrapped her arms around his neck, her legs climbing his frame until he pulled his head back and said, "Whoa."

He gently disentangled himself, feeling his blood pounding. Apparently, once his sex drive came back to life, there was just no shutting it off. He tried to cool down his mind, but his body refused to cooperate. He studied her, leaning against the fence, dealing with her own shock of withdrawal.

"I guess we are in a public place, aren't we?" she asked, her voice calm, thoughtful.

"Yeah, we sure are."

"Too bad. But now I think I need to run that off a little bit more."

And she bolted past him again. Swearing and laughing, he raced behind her. And that was the way it went for the next several blocks. Finally he caught up to her. "We are well past three miles."

She nodded. "I know. It just feels so damn good to get out here."

They looked around, then took off again, and when they hit the corner where her apartment building was, they slowed their steps and walked to cool down.

"How about we go out for breakfast?"

"I'm in. Shower first."

She turned her gaze to him. "Together?" Laughing, still chasing each other, he caught her once they were in the elevator. When the doors opened, she slipped out from under him, and he caught her again at the apartment door. By the time they made it inside, laughing, he called out a warning, "Don't forget the cameras."

Her laughter was shrill. She clapped a hand over her mouth. "Shower." And she bolted toward the bathroom.

He went into the bedroom and closed the door where he stripped off his clothes and headed into the shower behind her. He could get used to this. In a big way.

Chapter 11

AFTER SEVERAL DAYS with nothing else out of the ordinary, Kai wondered if they'd scared off her stalker. Then she remembered the note on the window. As she walked into the office, Tyson at her side, she said in a low voice, "Is he just waiting for us to make a move, to slack off our security, or do you think there's any chance you guys scared him away?"

"Probably the first two. But does that mean he's given up? I can't say."

"Neither can you sit here babysitting me all the time. As much as I love spending time with you, you can't just stay here forever. You have a job to do. And it's not babysitting me for nothing." She deliberately avoided looking at him. He wasn't getting paid to do this. That was fine and dandy for a day or two. But they were now five days in.

"I doubt he'll let it go much longer."

"Let what go much longer?"

"Let you off the hook for hanging around me. It's eating away at him, making him miserable and angry. Then he'll want to punish you for cheating on him."

Kai gave him an outraged look. "I what?"

He nodded. "You and I know that's not what you are doing. That doesn't mean he agrees with us."

"It's such a bizarre feeling to think somebody out there is

keeping track of my every move."

"But he is. Even if he's gone to ground for a few days."

"It's so damn frustrating. I want an enemy I can target, somebody you can go after. This hiding away in the background to jump out in the dark is not cool."

Tyson chuckled. "You sure you don't just want me gone?"

"Hell no. I wouldn't mind having a vacation where we could take off, really enjoy ourselves," she said, fluttering her eyelashes at him. "It's fun playing house, but there's always that pressure in the background."

"Hopefully he'll make a move soon."

She walked into the office to find a definite edge in the atmosphere. She frowned. Tommy was here but avoided looking at her. She walked over and asked him, "What's going on?"

He hunched his shoulders and said, "Please don't ask me."

She studied him for a long moment, glanced around and said, "Where is Warren?"

"In his office."

She knocked on the door twice but got no answer. When there was no sound from inside, she knocked again harder. The door was flung open, and Warren stood with anger in his face. "If I don't answer the door, maybe it's because I don't want to talk to you."

She stepped back, surprised at his anger. She studied his face. "What's going on?"

He thrust his chin at her. "You'll find out when my lawyer contacts you. Until then, leave me the hell alone." And he slammed the door in her face.

She stared at the door blankly, then turned to Tyson. "I

have no idea why he's upset."

With a quick look around, she realized the others studiously kept their faces focused on their desks. And she realized it probably had something to do with her ownership buyout. "Like I need this now," she said half under her breath. On the other hand, there was no good time.

"It needs to be solved one way or another," Tyson said quietly.

She snorted as they walked to her corner office. She turned on her computer, waited until it booted up and checked her email. Tyson stood behind her, not prying. She brought up her emails to see one from her lawyer with the terse message, *Call me.*

She pulled out her cell phone, dialed his number and walked over to the boardroom. With Tyson standing at the door, she sat down in the empty room and waited for her lawyer to answer. When he did, he burst out, "Why did you go to the media?"

Shocked, she said, "Go to the media with what?"

"You know. You completely destroyed your partner in the media, called him all kinds of names. I've been hearing about it all morning from his lawyer."

She stood, walked closer to Tyson. "What the hell are you talking about? I haven't spoken to any media."

Her lawyer was silent for a moment and asked, "Are you serious?"

"Yes, I'm serious. Maybe you should send me whatever it is I was supposed to have done. Because, as of right now, I don't know what you're talking about."

"Somebody hates you in a big way."

She froze, turned slowly to look at Tyson and said, "Well, somebody does hate me, but it's a police matter, and we certainly haven't been able to ID who it is."

Her lawyer's tone turned brisk. "Talk to me. Why haven't I heard about this before?"

"It's my stalker and didn't involve my company, so I didn't tell you about it," she said bluntly. "It's a police matter." She took a deep breath and explained further. When she finally ran out of words, she could almost hear the wheels of her lawyer's head turning.

"That explains it. Somebody's manipulating your life, that's for sure. I don't know how you can get out of this one because I doubt your partner will believe anything you say."

"Well, he should know better. It's also my company. Why would I do anything that would hurt our own sales?"

"I hear you. But his lawyer is pissed."

"I think it's his job to be pissed for no reason," she snapped in frustration. "I've got nothing to apologize for because I didn't do anything. The fact that I'm being targeted is not my fault." She hung up the phone and sat down in a boardroom chair. "Christ, this is so stupid."

With Tyson asking some pointed questions, she got the story out. As she finished, Warren strode across the floor.

"I want you to get the hell out of this building."

Tyson stepped between the two of them, his arms crossed.

Warren sneered. "Sure, go sleep with the help, why don't you? Just so you could get a bodyguard. You probably made all the shit up, just to bring more drama into your life. What you did this morning was completely off the wall."

She wanted to argue, but it didn't make any sense. She didn't know what she was supposed to have done, but she could imagine. "You are accusing me of having done something I didn't do, and now you won't listen to me."

"Because nothing you say will make me believe you."

She slowly said, "Then I guess it is time to dissolve our business association."

"You can buy me out," he said. "My lawyers are talking to your lawyer now."

She snorted. "Really? It might be a little hard to come up with that kind of money."

"Then we should shut down, and we'll both lose big time."

"So that means you're not interested in buying me out?"

He shook his head. "This was a failing company when you joined. We're a sinking ship right now. And after what you've done to it today, it's really not worth anything. I'm not taking any more losses. Same price you bought in, buy me out, or we have to dissolve it as it stands." Then Warren stalked back to his office, slamming his door.

Sounded like a lot of money lost and a lot of jobs out the windows. She sat, watching the sunrise for a long time. Finally she phoned her lawyer again and asked, "What's going on?"

"He's looking for a buyout. Same price you bought in."

"I don't have it," she said bluntly. "See if you can get back some of my investment." She hung up, stood and faced Tyson. "I need to go for a walk."

He never said a word. They walked back to her computer. She quickly logged out, shut it down, grabbed her purse and walked outside.

She walked for what seemed like hours, her mind stewing, trying to find a way through. Warren had likely been on the edge of doing this for a long time now. Since Mark's death. That Mark had left his shares to her had finished Warren. It had all come down at the same time, giving her the control that Warren had never planned on handing over—which was the final straw. She'd been fascinated with the potential the company had right from the beginning. And she certainly wasn't against being the sole owner, but getting there was a different issue. Warren wanted a buyout. But it was still more money than she had. Going to the bank for that kind of money was likely impossible as well.

She walked to a coffee shop, picked up two coffees, one for each them, and came back outside. "Thanks for walking with me," she said quietly as she took a seat at one of the outdoor tables.

He shrugged. "Sometimes it's the best thing we can do. Life isn't always fun or nice. Right now you apparently have a little more trouble than most people."

She nodded. "Since the stalker can't get at me personally, he's getting at me professionally. Very smart."

Tyson nodded slowly. "That would make sense."

She slouched back in her chair and stared off, her mind still not locking on to anything in particular. Another heavy sigh broke free. She reached up and rubbed her temple. "Well, it's not how I expected my day to go."

"It's been a rough week."

She gave a snort. "Yes, it has. But I can't see a way out of this one."

"That's because you're not looking."

Startled, she stared at him. "What did I miss?"

"A world full of money out there. Contact your investors."

"Oh, I've done that before. But today I don't have the means to put up any assets for collateral, nor do I really want any other partners after this mess with Warren. Unless he's willing to drop his price, I can't go it alone."

"Well, he sees his company as in trouble. He wants to sell, so a good lawyer will pressure him to take half of what he's asking for."

A text came in just then. She looked at it and said, "The lawyer again." She read the message. Basically what she already knew. She sent back a quick text. **I can't pull off that buy-out figure, but that's more doable. Pressure him into selling at half of that, but I'll still need some help raising the money.**

She hit Send and sat back. "Even at half of Warren's asking price, I sure don't have that kind of money."

"Do you know Logan?"

She frowned. "Yeah. His dad is a bigwig in the military."

Tyson nodded. "He's retired now."

She nodded. "Logan and Flynn were buddies."

"They still are."

"And why does it matter right now?"

"Logan's dad invests in all kinds of things."

She studied Tyson for a long moment. "Like loans?"

Tyson smiled. "It depends on which deal is better, as an investor or as a loan."

"I have no idea which way to go. There's a hell of a difference between having a business partner versus a loan payment."

He nodded. "I suggest we do something fun for the rest of the day. Give your mind a break."

She shook her head. "I can't do that. I have a bunch of phone calls to make, people to contact to smooth over whatever damage the media did today. Plus, I'm supposed to do a training session tomorrow, which I should probably cancel. Not to mention we have other tools I need to be pushing too."

"Have you checked your emails or text messages?"

"Only my lawyer's. I have his set to a certain ring tone so I know when he contacts me. The rest, well, it's been going off at a steady rate." At that, she picked up her phone, checked her Message screen and held it up so he could note her twenty-two unread messages.

He nodded. "Then let's go back to the office. Business is business. Whether it's rain or shine, it's still business."

Back at the office the staff was working hard and avoided looking at her. Warren's office door was locked, and the lights were out, so she turned to Tommy. "Has he left for the day?"

Tommy nodded.

She headed to her office, sat down and proceeded to get to work.

No one else said a word. It was a very uncomfortable few hours, but she had so much work to do, it didn't matter. She kept her head down and her focus on what she was doing. By the time she got through the emails and texts with apologies and simple explanations, she felt like somebody had put her through an old wringer washer. The entire time Tyson sat beside her on his phone.

She didn't have a clue what he was doing, but she had to trust he was doing something useful.

The staff stayed quiet, working with their heads down, focusing on their work, making her realize just how strained and awkward her work environment had become.

Did she want to keep the company? Could she work with these people? Tommy probably. Not sure of the others. Did she want to have their livelihoods in her hands? It was more than she needed to deal with right now. But, if that was the case, then what? What would she do? She'd put a ton of money into this company.

She couldn't afford to lose it, so she would continue limping along. And buy out Warren. Of course for a lot less now ...

At the end of the day, Tommy got up and walked out, followed by the other staff—as if they had waited to go as a group. She wanted to say goodbye, but, since they didn't say anything to her, she let them walk out in silence.

Her phone rang. "Hello, Levi." She sat back with a tired sigh and asked, "Any news?"

"No, but as a smear campaign goes, this one has been relatively short. I spoke to several people who said they'd heard rumors that your company was in financial trouble but didn't have any sources to back up the rumors." He cleared his throat. "We did find something odd. One person did say they heard that you might have had something to do with Mark's death."

Too shocked to speak, silence filled the phone until she said, "Dear God. He was my friend."

"And you gained his shares ..."

"How sad anybody would even consider that," she said. "People need to find something nice to focus on."

"Not going to happen as long as something juicy is there to chew on instead."

She gave a broken laugh, but inside her heart broke to think anyone could say that about her and Mark. "Well, hopefully this will die out fast too, and I can go back to being anonymous. This kind of directed attention is not my thing."

Levi's tone was quiet and empathetic as he said, "No, none of us wants to have the spotlight turned on us like this." After a pause, he said, "Tyson said this has caused a breach in your partnership. Is that correct?"

"You could say that. But obviously there has been a crack in the relationship for a long time. Warren didn't like how he had to sell out to me. But he could live with it as he still had a controlling interest. When Mark died, I got his shares and the balance of power shifted. Warren's attitude changed completely. Then he became quite negative and disruptive."

"Any chance he did any of this?" Levi asked. "We're checking into Warren and Mark's relationship. And still investigating Mark's accident."

Her eyes popped open. "I don't know," she said. "I don't know why he would. He stands to make a lot of money if we can hold this company together and move forward."

"But, if he doesn't like the corporate structure, doesn't believe in you and the situation he's gotten himself into, maybe he just wants out."

She leaned back and rubbed her neck. "It's possible. I just don't know how I can come up with that kind of money."

"Another reason I'm calling. I spoke to Gunner. I don't know if you know him."

"Logan's father. Tyson mentioned him."

"Yeah, he wants to meet with you. At least talk to you. Look at options."

"I'm not sure I'm ready to take on another investor," she said slowly. "I put a lot of my heart and soul into this company last year. It's really shitty timing."

"Maybe, and maybe he'd give you a loan instead. That would be the best. The product you guys came up with is huge. I know men who would like to invest. But, if you don't want investors, I get it."

"I have no idea at this point," she said. "I have to talk to a few people and see what's the best way to go."

"Talk to Gunner. I trust him. He wouldn't rip you off. He's been around the block a few times. You could use the advice right now."

She thanked Levi and put her phone on the desk. "Gunner wants to talk to me."

Tyson glanced at her in surprise. "You know? That's one of the things I like about Levi. Something gets mentioned, and, no questions asked, he is on it. He's a doer, not just a thinker."

She gave a slow smile. "Is Gunner trustworthy?"

"I've never done business with him directly, so I can't say. But I've never heard anything other than good words about him."

She looked at the name and number Levi had given her. "I guess it can't hurt to talk to the man." She called and was transferred to Gunner immediately. Under the circumstances, all agreed to a short phone conversation for the moment. When she hung up, she stood and said, "Gunner's got good insights. I'll consider some of his suggestions. For now I need to get out of here."

"Good timing. It's after six anyway."

"Really?" She checked her watch and shook her head. "Well, I didn't expect that. I had no idea so much time had gone by."

"That happens when you're having fun," Tyson said with a smile as he stood and waited for her to collect her stuff. He wandered around the other desks. "Do you know these men's histories? Do you know anything about them? Before buying into the company, did you research the intellectual property of the owners and employees? The brainpower working for a company is important. Did you know one of them used to be military?"

She nodded. "Larry, I think."

"He was a paratrooper, and, according to a lot of people I contacted about him, he was very good at getting in and out of places he wasn't supposed to."

Her footsteps faltered as she made her way to the front door. She turned and looked at him. "As in that note on my living room window? As in getting into my bedroom?"

"Both are possible. What if this wasn't about stalking you personally? What if it was more a case of Warren and Larry working together to get *you* to sell out? Hoping you'd ask him to buy you out at a serious discount so you could leave town?"

"He didn't have the money then. How would he have any now? Besides he's never said anything to me about it."

"You don't know where he sits financially. And that might have been the original plan until something changed. Let's just ask Ice to look into Warren's current financial status. It might explain why he now wants to sell."

She shook her head. "I'm not following you. How does any of this explanation make sense? Why create the ugly media storm?"

"Maybe to increase the pressure on you?" Tyson shrugged. "To devalue the company? He needed money before, so he was forced to accept you as a co-owner. But, when you took over Mark's shares, that business relationship has quickly deteriorated. Now that you have a stalker, maybe he thought you'd gladly sell and leave town. Now that the police are involved, any number of other issues could arise, including background checks into him and his personal life. Maybe he realizes he's in danger of getting caught for having done something criminal. And now he just wants out. If he can get you to buy him out at the same rate that you paid last time, he can take his money and run. With any luck, he could avoid jail time too for whatever he's done."

She turned to stare at Warren's office. "You think he got Larry to help?"

"Or what if he got Larry's help in the beginning, only his help took on a life of its own?"

She stared at Tyson. "Oh, boy. That's …"

He nodded. "It's all conjecture. But nothing has been normal about Warren's behavior. And now that we know he has somebody working for him with the skills necessary to do everything that's been done so far …"

"You'll check to see if Larry has a criminal record? If he's ever been in any kind of difficulties with girlfriends, ever had any kind of assault charges dropped, anything like that?"

"Levi and Ice are looking into it further. And his military record. We'll get answers soon," Tyson promised.

She shook her head. "It won't be soon enough." They walked out of the office, turned and locked it behind them. She stood at the door and said, "We can access Warren's computer, you know. I do own fifty-one percent of the company. Everything in there is mine, in terms of getting any information off the hard drives."

Tyson gave her a ghost of a smile. "Already in progress."

She groaned. "Maybe I don't want to know."

At that he laughed and led her out into the sunshine. "Maybe you don't."

AS LONG AS developments were ongoing, Kai had no need to get too worried about the lack of progress. But Tyson had to admit he wanted to get the asshole stalking her. Warren was Tyson's prime suspect, but just because he was extremely disagreeable didn't mean he was the guilty party.

"Are we going home to cook? Or do you want to go to a restaurant? Or shall we pick up a picnic and head someplace quiet?"

"The last one," she said immediately. "Maybe that will still the noise in my mind."

"No, it won't. But it might help calm it down."

They walked to a sandwich place a couple blocks away, ordered what they each wanted. A small grocery store was next door where Tyson picked up several pieces of fruit and bottles of water. Back at the vehicle Tyson said, "You okay if I drive?"

She nodded and got into the passenger side with the to-go bags. "If you have a place in mind, then let's go there."

He had a couple places. He chose one less traveled, but knew Levi and Ice could track the vehicle and would know where they were. When he pulled up to the small empty parking lot, he motioned toward the water in front of them. "I found this place just after I arrived."

"Perfect." She grabbed their meal, her sweater, locked her purse in the glove box and hopped out. They walked to the water's edge and sat down. She tilted her face toward the sun and smiled. "I thought things were going so well until today."

"Shit happens for no reason. And you just have to make your way through it."

She gurgled with laughter and turned to look at him. "Now that's a good saying."

He gave her a lopsided grin, loving the brightness in her expression coming back. It was tough to see somebody you cared about sink into quagmires of stress. "And, if you're up for it, at least consider what Logan's father could do for you."

"I have to talk to my investment advisor to see what he says too." She stared mutely at the water, picked up a small rock beside her and tossed it into the surface. As she watched the ripples spread outward, she said, "I knew Warren wouldn't be the easiest to deal with, but Mark was great, so I figured it was worth it. Then Mark died ..."

"I know."

"It makes no sense that Warren would want out right now," she said. "If you think about it, we have a good product. Once we take it to the game market, it'll be massive. Why does Warren want to get out before he makes a ton of money?"

She had a good point. One he couldn't quite come up with an answer to. "You know what's going on in his personal life?"

She shook her head. "He divorced a couple years ago, pitched a fit because of the settlement, and he's had a couple girlfriends but nothing serious since."

Tyson frowned. "I think we need to understand his motive. It's possible he's being threatened. It's possible your stalker got to both of you. But that would certainly not fit the mold of a generic stalker."

"I'm so afraid something is wrong with the software on one of the products, or we don't own the patents we're supposed to. That a house of cards is about to collapse in my face."

He looked at her sharply. "You need to find out fast. Because, if he knows something like that and isn't telling you ..."

She nodded, pulled out her phone and sent her lawyer a detailed message. When done, she dropped the phone beside her and said, "God, I hate this shit."

He linked her fingers with his. "How about chewing on the problems by eating something? Give the acid in your stomach something else to work on besides itself."

She stared at the packages beside her. "Do you remember whose sandwich was whose?"

He pulled out one with her initials on the top and handed it to her. She opened it and took several bites. "Oh, my gosh, this is good," she moaned. She glanced at his. "Yours is laced with jalapenos. How could you possibly taste the rest of the ingredients?" .

He couldn't answer as his mouth was full. When he finished the bite and swallowed, he said, "I love spicy food."

"I like spicy food as long as some flavor still goes with the heat."

When he'd eaten most of his sandwich, he reached for a bottle of water and took a big swig. His phone rang. He pulled it out and pressed the Speaker button. "Levi, what's up?"

"Warren is planning to leave the country. He's booked flights out of Dallas in six days."

Kai's eyebrows shot up. "Why not Houston?"

"No idea. The bigger question is, where is he going?" Tyson said.

"Per his office computer he's been searching for data on living as an ex-pat in Thailand and also for disappearing completely," Levi said.

"What if the company doesn't own one of the patents it's supposed to own, or something illegal is going on?"

"We're tugging those lines and will call if we find something," Levi said. "But does that make him the stalker?"

"Not necessarily. Not if he's trying to leave the country," Tyson said.

"A lot of buy-out money is at stake," Kai added. "Something very serious must be going on if he's leaving without getting his money back."

When Levi hung up, Kai could feel the fear coming off her shoulders in waves. "Holy crap. Did I really make a bad investment?"

"Did you do your due diligence research?"

She nodded. "Definitely. But, if Warren's a lying, cheating, stealing fraud, then maybe I missed something."

"Give Levi a chance to dig around. It's not the first time he's seen things like this." Tyson shrugged. "At this point it is just guesses though."

"And that's very frustrating," she said.

He nodded, handing her a bottle of water. "You're not alone. Remember that."

With the news from Levi, Tyson had to admit too many bad options were possibly working right now that they weren't even aware of yet. And he wasn't feeling terribly comfortable with any of them. Warren was a sleazebag, but that didn't make him a criminal. If he was involved, something had spooked him. There was no other reason to sell his shares, take less than they were worth, right before a huge payday. Fear was a hell of a motivator. Guys like Warren were weak and easy to manipulate. So the real question was, what the hell was really going on with the stalker? And did Warren have anything to do with it?

She bounced to her feet and was suddenly at his side. "Let's walk. I feel like a sitting duck here."

He packed up their garbage and headed with her to walk

the path. He kept watch but saw nothing.

As they neared the parking lot, he heard a single hard *crack*. Immediately he tucked her behind him, and they pressed up against a group of trees.

"Now my stalker has a gun?" Kai whispered.

"But so do I," Tyson said in a hard voice. He reached down and pulled out a small handgun out of his ankle holster and handed it to her. "Now so do you."

She stared at it for a long moment, then snatched it out of his hand. "Damn. When I left the military I'd hoped this life was over."

"The way the world is these days, that life might never be over. If you don't have a handgun use my spare until we can get you one." He searched their surroundings but found nothing out of the ordinary. "He's escalating, like we thought he would." Through the woods he spotted their SUV, alone in the parking lot. No one else was around. They waited, but nothing more happened. Telling Kai to stay put, he raced to the vehicle for a closer look. He called Levi. "Someone shot out one of the tires."

"Damn. Stay hidden," he said. "Calvary's coming."

Staying hidden wasn't exactly what he wanted to do, but no way could he leave Kai alone. He couldn't take that chance. There was no way to know if the shooter was working alone or had someone coming up behind them even now. He raced back to her. "Levi's coming. The vehicle has a tire shot out."

She looked pale but didn't say a word. That was something else he really liked about her. She was good people—solid, dependable, never got into a frenzy during an emergency.

On the highway he caught sight of a vehicle on the

shoulder. He motioned toward it, asking if she could make out more than the fact it was a truck.

She studied it, then shook her head. "Just a truck to me."

He pulled out his phone and called Ice. "A truck's sitting on the highway just past the turnoff to the park. Can you bring it up on satellite and get an ID?" He studied the horizon, catching sight of another rooftop. "There is also a car."

"On it. Levi should be there within ten minutes," Ice said.

"Was he in town?"

"He's been in town most of the day," she said. "Found them. Now I'll work on getting the license plates." Then she said suddenly, "Have to go."

He put away his phone. "Ice confirmed a car and a truck are up there. She's trying to get an ID on both."

"Any chance my stalker hijacked the GPS on Levi's SUV and is following us?"

"He doesn't really have to. He put his own tracker on it. I found it yesterday."

She spun and stared at him with outrage. "You didn't tell me."

He turned a flat stare at her. "What was the point? You have enough to worry about."

Chapter 12

STILL SMARTING AT being left out of the information loop, Kai watched from the hiding place in the trees as Tyson approached the vehicles parked on the side of the highway. She hadn't seen them in the first place. But with Levi and Jace here to aid Tyson, they wanted to check out the area.

She stood out of the way as the men walked, took photographs of the tracks, moved forward and studied the ground. For all her military experience, she didn't have this tracking knowledge that the guys seemed to use. She wondered if that had more to do with their SEAL training.

Women still weren't allowed to be part of that elite group, but she knew times were changing. One of these days, a woman would be a SEAL. She wondered if it would be all that the first woman expected it to be. It was one of the last male bastions to be breached. She couldn't imagine many on either side would take it lightly. Not that SEALs were sexist, but it was like the supreme male territory. On the other hand, if the woman could do the job and they trusted her, the men would be fine with it. Just look at Ice.

Tyson walked toward Kai and said, "We can leave now."

"Are they coming with us?" she asked as she walked to the passenger side.

"We're heading to the compound to get more clothes for

me and to see if Ice found out anything more."

Surprised about the visit to Levi's compound, but totally okay with the idea, she closed and locked the door beside her.

"I've known Levi for a long time now," Tyson said quietly. "And I just started working for him, but I'm still amazed at what he can accomplish."

She nodded. "He's a bit of a legend. I suppose you know Mason too?"

At that Tyson's face split with a big grin. "Who the hell doesn't know Mason's merry band of keepers?"

She chuckled. "The thing is, I think most men are getting into his unit so they can become one of the merry band."

"That's funny. Levi's afraid he's got the same thing happening with his group."

"You know," she turned to look at him and said, "at one point, you would've been more than happy to be included in that group."

"Absolutely. When Tracy was around, I felt like I was a keeper. Felt like I was one of the chosen."

"And now?" she asked curiously. "What's changed?"

He shrugged. "Anything and everything. And yet, at the same time, nothing."

Taking that as an excuse to exit that conversation, she settled back to watch the countryside whip past them. "What's it like living on the compound?"

"Ask me in six months when I've really had a chance to experience it."

"Right, this is all new to you. What about Michael and Jace?"

"Both of them are new too."

After that there wasn't a whole lot more to say, so she stayed quiet. Several messages came in from her lawyer but no solution as yet. "My lawyer says he had a discussion with Warren's lawyer, but they're waiting on Warren to answer some questions."

"Is he capable of answering questions?"

Startled she shot him a look. "What do you mean?"

"The man is running. There's a reason why. If it's enough for him to sell everything and leave the country, there's a good chance he's in danger. As in serious danger."

Her jaw dropped. "I figured he was just being a cowardly weasel, abandoning ship as it sunk."

He shook his head. "I'm pretty sure we'll find it's a whole lot more than that."

"You're not suggesting he hasn't answered his emails because he can't, are you?"

"I don't know. But I think on our way home tonight, if he still hasn't answered, we run by his place and see."

Just then they turned off the highway and drove past Anna's Animal Rescue Center and honked lightly twice as everyone did, letting her know it was them.

"I haven't heard too much about the center. It's Flynn's place, isn't it?"

"It's Anna's. She's Flynn's lady. She works to rehabilitate the animals for adoption."

"That's admirable," Kai said softly. "It's not fair how the animals take the brunt of human ugliness."

"No, it's not. And she is doing her part. I'm told Levi's group takes turns helping out when we can."

She glanced at him and laughed. "Really? That's nice."

He gave her a grin. "I haven't been there long enough, but, since she's a nonprofit, working off donations only, I can see there might be times when she needs a helping hand from volunteers."

"And Flynn's really good friends with Logan?"

"Right, and that leads us back to Gunner again."

She settled in as the compound came into view. "Levi's got quite the place here."

"He does indeed." Tyson drove in and parked. "I need to grab more clothing while I'm here."

"I gather you think I can't be alone for a while yet?" she joked as she exited the SUV.

"Not until we settle this," Levi said from beside her. He'd approached so silently she hadn't heard him arrive.

She turned to look at him. "Remember, I can't pay you for all this."

"We didn't ask. Sometimes we just have to help our own."

She opened her arms and gave him a big hug. "Thank you. That's the nicest thing anybody's said to me in a long time."

Levi wrapped an arm around her shoulders and led her inside. "I know you guys just ate, but I'm pretty sure Alfred is getting ready to serve dessert."

"Perfect," Kai said. "If I'm lucky, Tyson might share some with me."

Levi snorted. "It's not Tyson we have to worry about. Have you seen how much Stone eats?"

As they walked in, they found Stone sitting down to a rather large piece of cheesecake. He looked up guiltily, saw who it was and gave them a big grin. "It's the last piece."

Levi froze and then swore at him.

Stone chuckled. "Gotcha." He motioned to the other end of the table where a huge cheesecake waited. "Like

Alfred would let me have the last piece," he scoffed.

Ice walked out of the kitchen with two plates of cheesecake in her hand. She held one out to Levi.

Kai watched in fascination at this personal glimpse into their lives. She sat down beside Stone. "It amazes me you can eat this amount of food."

He looked at her with wide eyes and a smile. "I have to keep up my strength. My Lissa doesn't like it if I get too skinny."

A beautiful blonde laughed on the other side of Stone. The woman leaned forward. "I'm Lissa."

"Kai." When Kai turned back to the table, she saw Tyson plunk down two plates of cheesecake, one in front of her and one for himself. He motioned at the coffeepot on the sideboard. "There's coffee if you want." And then he sat down and proceeded to tuck into his cheesecake like he hadn't eaten in a month.

She realized that, given the amount of food he must eat here on a regular basis, he had been on short rations at her place.

Just then Alfred walked through with a big smile on his face.

"Alfred, your homemade jam," Tyson said when he could talk around the mouthful, "gives this that extra something."

"And I love doing it," Alfred said. "It's even easier now that I have help."

Another woman walked in from the kitchen carrying two large coffeepots and walked around the table, topping off every coffee cup. "Hi. I'm Bailey. I just missed your visit the other day."

"You mean, when my life was normal?" Kai said jokingly.

Bailey nodded as she set the fresh coffeepots on the sideboard, took out the two older ones, putting the fresh ones in their place.

"No, it wasn't," Tyson said as he placed his fork on the empty plate. "It was a long way from normal, but you were keeping busy, ignoring the problem." He glanced at her plate. "You going to eat that?"

She gave him a frown, studied the empty plate in front of him and pulled her plate closer. "Yes, I so am."

"Well fine." He gave an exaggerated sigh and sat back. "But if it's too much ..."

She gave him a look of outrage. "You can always ask Alfred for a second piece."

He gave her a crafty look but stayed quiet.

She shook her head as she worked the angles to getting more cheesecake and quickly took her first bite. Then she stopped and moaned. "Oh, my God, this is like, what? White chocolate?"

"White chocolate almond," Bailey said cheerfully. "One of my favorite recipes."

"Man, how did you guys get lucky enough to find Bailey and Alfred?" Before she knew it, her dessert was gone too. "I could almost eat a second piece myself."

Bailey stopped beside her. "Would you like a second?"

"Yes, thanks."

Ice sat down beside Kai. "We've tracked the truck back to the city into a very large car park. The license plate led us to a vehicle that the owner, who is out of town, didn't know was missing. However, when we went to look for it, it was no longer there. That car park does have several entrances and exits, and I did not see it leaving, but I don't have access to the other side."

"So we're no farther ahead than before."

Tyson nodded. "The car?"

"A middle-aged couple drove it farther down to a different spot in the park. They parked, got out and, the last I looked, they were still sitting on a bench, holding hands."

"Both dead ends. How lovely."

Levi spoke up from the other side of the table. "Warren, on the other hand …"

Kai turned to look at Levi.

"He's in great financial distress and needs cash. So he does need to sell his shares. He has sold his apartment and would have raised a decent amount from that when it closed."

"He sold his apartment?" she cried out in astonishment. "I had no idea. He must have been planning this for a while then."

Levi nodded. "And his money all disappeared from his bank account in one day. Tracking it, however, is not quite so easy."

She settled back. "I didn't have a clue. He never mentioned anything." She glanced at Tyson. "Any idea what he's up to?"

"I think he's connected to your stalker."

Everyone at the table turned to stare at him.

"In what way?" Ice asked.

"I don't have any proof, but there is no reason for him to run *unless* he's connected, or he's done something equally fraudulent in terms of company business."

"I spoke to Gunner," Levi said. "He hasn't heard any rumblings about Warren. No alerts or any history of fraudulent dealings."

"I don't understand a whole lot in the corporate business world," Kai admitted. "So it's nice to know I can talk to Gunner about things."

"I told him about the product we're testing for you. He was very interested, and he has an awful lot of clientele who would be interested in a similar system."

She brightened. "It's a good product, isn't it?"

Tyson interjected, "It's one of the best we've seen. In other words, we want to keep your business." He covered her hand with his. "Your business took a hit today, but Warren is not the company. You and your projects are."

TYSON DROVE AS they left the compound and headed toward Warren's apartment.

"If he sold it a couple weeks ago, where's he staying now?" Kai asked.

"The sale closes tomorrow. So he could still be clearing out the place now, if he hasn't already done that. He could be staying at a hotel until the sale clears," Tyson said. "We have to take a chance he's still there. It wouldn't hurt for the two of you to talk."

"I'm sure both our lawyers have already done that."

"Gotta love lawyers …" Tyson said, a note of humor in his voice. "If this has nothing to do with you and your stalker, then obviously something else is going on that maybe some honest communication would fix."

She sighed. "I agree. I'm just not sure Warren will talk to me."

"Would he stay with one of the guys who work for you?"

"I don't think so, but I don't know what their relationship is outside of work. Maybe they are all good buddies. I don't know."

The drive back to Houston was quiet, just the sound of the wheels racing through the night. "Do you want music on?"

"No," she murmured. "It's nice to have the peace and quiet."

As Tyson approached the outskirts of town, he punched Warren's address into the GPS and it gave them a route.

She studied it. "His apartment isn't very far from me," she exclaimed. "I didn't know that."

"Does it matter?"

She shook her head. "No, not at all. Just makes him a little more accessible than I had thought."

"That also makes you a little more accessible to him," he said with a hard gaze.

"He's more weaselly than scary."

Tyson nodded. "That might be, but stalkers don't look like stalkers. Who knows what yours looks like."

She nodded. "Let's check out Warren's home and see."

Tyson parked on the front access street, and together they got out. Holding hands, they approached Warren's apartment building. She called Warren but got no response. She called again. "You think he's already left town? Like you said, the sale closes tomorrow. So he has to be out at noon at the latest."

Tyson stepped back and looked up at the apartments, figuring out which would be Warren's apartment. Just then somebody walked down and opened the door.

Kai stepped forward. "Thank you."

The man walked away without a care as to what stranger he had just let into the building.

Tyson shook his head and joined her in the hall. He

glanced around but didn't see any security. "This building's a similar age and state to yours."

"Meaning?"

"Meaning, I doubt any video cameras are set up here."

"Maybe that doesn't matter." She shrugged.

Tyson motioned toward the stairs. "Let's walk up."

"I guess I could use the exercise after that cheesecake, right?" She laughed lightly and raced upstairs ahead of him. He followed slower, his eyes checking for security cameras. But he couldn't see any. So no way to keep track of when Warren went home or left. Or if he'd had any visitors.

On the fourth floor, Kai pulled open the double doors, and they stepped into the hallway. Geometric patterns of multiple browns filled the hall leading to various apartments. Tyson walked to number 462 and knocked. No answer.

He knocked again, placing his ear against the door. Nothing. He turned the knob. To his surprise, the door pushed open. He nudged it wider with his foot. Hearing Kai gasp, he held a finger to his lips, but he knew from the look in her eyes that she understood. Warren might've been running for his life, but Tyson didn't think Warren had been fast enough.

Leaving Kai in the hall, Tyson took several steps inside.

Boxes were all over the living room floor. They were taped and labeled. From the labels he could see, it looked like the boxes were going to Goodwill. The walls were empty; furniture was gone. Warren really was booking it. Tyson quickly stepped into the kitchen, which was spotless. It looked like Warren hadn't ever cooked here.

Tyson filed away that little tidbit in case it was needed later and kept walking through the apartment. The bedroom had no bed, no dresser; the room was empty. Not even boxes remained. But the smell ... He quickly stepped into the small bathroom and found the missing owner. Warren was scrunched up in the bathtub, covered in blood.

Both his wrists had been slashed. Tyson stood for a long moment studying the body, realizing it was meant to look like a suicide, except for one thing. The cuts went from the inside of the wrists to the outside. Suicides always went from the outside of the wrists to the inside. It was the only way they could slice when self-inflicted.

This was murder.

He pulled out his phone and called Levi. "We've got a problem."

Chapter 13

KAI LEANED AGAINST the bathroom door, her hand over her mouth. She stared at Warren's body in shock. She'd seen dead bodies before. But none had been friends, business partners or coworkers. She could feel the scream clawing up her throat. She stamped it down firmly. This wasn't the time or the place. She'd had enough military experience to know how to keep her emotions under control.

But her military experience had nothing to do with this reality. Besides, her experience had been as a no-holds-barred trainer and weapons trainer. She'd never been in active missions. As she looked at the bloody mess in the bathtub, she realized that may have been a good thing.

She'd always thought she'd missed out on something. But she had heard enough tales from so many returning soldiers that she'd realized it was a whole lot less glamorous than the posters made it sound. She did her best to train the soldiers so they were as well-equipped as they possibly could be before they headed out to the front line.

Tyson stepped in front of her, deliberately blocking her view of Warren. Tyson placed a hand on her shoulder, giving her a gentle squeeze with his fingers. "You okay?"

She stared up at him blankly. "Yes, I'm fine. Did he really do this to himself?"

Tyson gave a decisive shake of his head. "No, he did not.

This is definitely murder."

The words stuck in her throat. She stared at him, her eyes rounding in shock. "Murder?" she whispered, her voice dropping to just barely discernible. "Are you sure?"

He nodded. "The killer cut Warren's wrists the wrong way."

She frowned and studied the gash. "Warren often did things backward," she said. "Maybe that was instinctive for him."

Tyson shook his head. "I doubt it. And I don't want to touch anything." He gently eased her out so she no longer leaned against the doorjamb. He motioned for her to turn and walk out of the apartment.

"But why kill him? Or why kill himself?" The idea of suicide was easier to handle than murder. Both were ugly. But one didn't involve yet another person.

"If it was suicide, maybe he could see his world crumbling and couldn't find a way to get out of it. If it was murder, it was to shut him up."

At the front door he gently pushed her into the hall. "I need a few moments in here to check out a couple things. Levi is on his way."

She frowned at him. "I could've stayed inside," she said quietly.

"Better that you're not in here any longer than you need to be."

She leaned against the wall, thinking about his statement, realizing that, if Warren's death really was murder, she would be one of the main suspects. Under her breath she whispered, "Jesus." As his business partner and with their contentious relationship well known, the police would consider her first.

Speaking of business relationships … She walked a few steps away and called her lawyer. "John, I'm at Warren's house."

"Oh, good. Did you come to an agreement?"

Her lips trembled at his cheerful voice. "Unfortunately, no. And there won't be one." She took a deep breath, hearing the puzzled silence on the other end. "He's dead, John."

"What? What happened?"

"He's in the bathtub. His wrists are slashed. I don't know if he committed suicide or if its murder."

"Jesus."

She rubbed her temple and walked to the end of the hall where she could stare out the window and keep an eye on the door in case Tyson came out. "I know. It looks bad no matter which way. Either he did this because of the problems with the company, or somebody did this to him, and I'll be one of the main suspects."

"I'll start the paperwork. Right now the company's in a delicate balance. I'll contact his lawyer and see where the land lies. I don't know what this loss entails yet, but you know this changes everything, right?"

"Nobody knows he's dead. We've called the police, but they haven't arrived yet."

"You're sure? You're absolutely certain it's him?"

She couldn't quite catch the sob breaking from her throat when she answered, "It's him. I saw him in the bathtub. Jesus, John, it's really Warren."

His voice softened. "Okay, take it easy."

After he hung up, she returned her phone to her pocket and stood with her arms wrapped around her chest, trying to get control of herself. What a mess. The rest of the staff would have to be told, and she had no idea what was going on behind the scenes with the company. She and Warren had both taken out life insurance policies in case something like this happened, but she had no clue if that covered suicide or murder. She assumed each partner was only covered if the cause of death was either natural or accidental.

She leaned against the window ledge as she waited for Tyson to come back out. But instead, Levi opened the door to the stairwell and appeared. He took one look at her and walked over with his arms open. She walked into them, accepting his warmth for a long moment.

"Tyson says it looks like murder," she whispered. "You need to know Warren was one of those guys who did things in an awkward way. It just worked for him." She tried hard to explain how sometimes he did things in reverse. How occasionally he used his left hand versus his right hand. She knew her explanation was garbled.

Levi gave her a gentle hug before stepping back. "Don't worry about it. There will be a lot more to the evidence than just that. We will get to the bottom of this."

She took a deep breath, feeling marginally better. "Thank you for coming."

He nodded, pulled a pair of gloves from his pocket, put them on and then, using his elbow, pushed the apartment door open. Tyson greeted him.

She leaned against the wall and waited. How long would they need?

Just as she wondered if she should say something, she saw a detective coming her way. She motioned toward the open door. "Tyson and Levi are in there."

A frown settled on his forehead, but he didn't say anything to her. Instead, he went inside. This time the door was closed with a harsh *click*. She heard voices but no yelling. She doubted the detective was happy as they preferred to be first on scene. But obviously somebody had to discover the body, and that somebody was supposed to stay until the police arrived.

Confused, distraught and not sure what she was supposed to do, she let herself slump to the floor where she sat with her knees to her chest and waited.

Finally the door opened, and Tyson stepped out, his gaze zooming to her. He squatted in front of her. "Are you ready to go?"

She gave a half snort. "I've been waiting like a zombie for the last hour. I'm well past ready to go. Did you learn anything new?"

He helped her to her feet. "Home," he said firmly. "We can talk when we get there."

She gave him a sharp look, but then remembered the tracker on the vehicle. Maybe he was worried about somebody overhearing the conversation.

When they got back to her apartment, she unlocked the door, walked in and tossed her phone on the counter beside her purse. Coming in behind her, Tyson held a small device in his hand she hadn't realized he had brought with him.

With a finger to his lips, he did a quick search of her apartment, looking for bugs. He checked her purse and phone as well and checked his cell too. When it came back all clear, he shut down the device. "Sorry about that, but I had to make sure."

"You're certain it's murder and not suicide?"

"The coroner'll make that determination. By my and Levi's vote, it's murder."

Her shoulders sagged. She'd been hoping against hope

that Warren had just been despondent over something in his personal life and had taken this as the best solution. If he had been murdered, it meant another bogeyman was out there. Chances were good it would connect to her.

"I suppose you didn't see or find anything that would give us a road map to his killer," she said, fatigue in her voice.

"Of course not," he said in a neutral tone.

She walked over to the coffeemaker and put on a pot. She certainly wasn't hungry, but she needed her cup of coffee.

"That would be way too easy."

She nodded. "Will you be involved in the investigation?" She turned to look at him in time to see his head shake.

"No. Detective Mannford is taking over now."

"Where is Levi?"

"Probably passing along what he knows about the case. Both cases have just dovetailed."

"A stalker is not a murderer."

"A stalker often starts off as a stalker and then becomes a murderer."

She froze, dropped her hands against the counter and bowed her head. "Is this really happening?"

"It really is. Have you contacted your lawyer?"

She brushed the tendrils of hair off her face and turned toward Tyson again. "Yes. I let him know about Warren's death, and I told him not to tell anybody else. But this will be a hell of a nightmare for the staff."

"Any idea where the company will end up with Warren's death?"

"I was trying to figure that out, but I didn't ask my lawyer directly. I think Warren's business partner insurance pays out if he died by natural causes or an accident, but I don't know what happens if it is suicide or murder." She walked into the living room, collapsed on the couch, curling up in a corner. "When do I tell the guys?"

"Not until we're given the okay."

She nodded. "Nobody's at work for the next two days anyway, so that's a short grace period."

"And I wouldn't contact any of the staff until the weekend is over."

Her gaze zeroed in on his face. "You really think they might be involved?"

"I can't rule anyone out," he said quietly. "Think about it. Someone had access to Warren's apartment and his computer. Someone had access to your phone. That leaves some very visible suspects."

"Remember how I inherited Mark's shares? That's what set Warren off. He thought he'd get them."

Tyson nodded.

"You realize the police could look to me for Warren's death." Tears threatened. She forced them back down.

"Except for one thing."

She frowned up at him. "What's that?"

"You've been with me for the last five days. You have a solid alibi. You did not kill Warren, and I can attest to that fact."

Inside she felt something settle at his words. She let out a heavy breath, releasing a tangled knot of tension from her shoulders. She nodded. "That's right. I forgot about that."

He smiled. "Well, I didn't. Mannford knows that too. The police will ask you questions that you're not going to like answering about yourself, Warren and your employees. Also about the current business fights over the media kerfuffle and Warren wanting to shut you out of the business. All of it."

"I will answer as best I can. But, in some ways, the detective would be better off talking to the lawyers."

"Don't worry. He will. The police will look at the legal issues between the two of you partners." He paused, then added quietly, "Make that the three of you."

"So Mark could have been murdered too?"

Tyson didn't answer, just stared at her.

She really didn't need a confirmation now. Unsettled and restless, she got up and walked around the living room. "Is there something we can do?"

"Yes. Make sure the murderer doesn't have a chance to find another target—like you."

TYSON POURED A cup of coffee for each of them. He handed her one. "I know there's no point in telling you not to worry."

She snorted. "How can I not? If it's the same man, he went from a stalker to a murderer. If it's not the same man, then we have two unknown people to worry about."

He contemplated her face for a long moment. "Well, at first I suspected Warren and Larry were working together. Now I have to revise that theory. Yet, I still wonder if two people are working together on this."

Startled, she said, "It fits the most recent events. Larry, being a former paratrooper, is capable of placing that message on my second-floor window, but I'd suspect the murderer shot out our tire."

He frowned, staring off into the distance. "Levi will call soon with an update from Mannford. I'll see what I can find in the meantime."

She placed her cup on the coffee table and flung herself

to the couch. "I hate being helpless. If it's one-on-one combat, you know I can hold my own."

He grinned. "Absolutely you can. My money's on you over a run-of-the-mill stalker any day," he said calmly. "But, if there's two of them involved or if he's a sniper or if he catches you by surprise with a Taser or chloroform or knockout drugs or multiple weapons, the fight is over before it starts. And you know that."

"This isn't supposed to happen to somebody like me. I'm a specialist in so many different martial art forms. I was an instructor in the military, and yet here I am, needing a bodyguard. I feel so stupid, like a fraud."

"We know perfectly well how good your skills are. If somebody decides they want to challenge you head-on, that's one thing. But what if they decide you need a handicap to even the fight, and they break your knees first?"

She nodded, her tone grim. "I know. I was thinking of that. In the military I ran a specific course on how to save your life when severely injured."

"And what was the advice you gave the recruits?"

Her voice was hard when she said, "Tactical retreat. Some battles you just can't win, no matter what. What you try to do is get away before they come in for the finishing kill."

He reached out an open hand. She slid hers into it, and he tugged her into his arms. "Between us, we've had the best training Uncle Sam can give us. We're smart, and there's two of us."

She nodded. "And yet I feel like, whoever this is, he's dancing around us, laughing his fool head off."

"Because he probably is. But the noose is tightening. And he's making mistakes."

"I like the sound of mistakes. What kind of mistake was made?"

"Killing Warren. If the murderer had left Warren alive, he would've been a great avenue to pursue for answers. But now that he's dead, his life will become an open book. Everyone will dissect his history, his bank accounts, every financial transaction he's made in the last twenty years, every relationship he's had, every step he's taken. Because you can bet this murderer is part of Warren's history. It's not just about keeping you safe. It's also now looking for justice for Warren. Regardless of what he did or did not do as part of this mess, he didn't deserve to be killed."

Her face brightened. "You're right. I'm just not thinking straight. I should've realized that now, with an open murder investigation, Warren's entire life will be completely ripped apart to find out what happened."

Tyson nodded, holding her close. "Not only just by Detective Mannford. Don't forget Levi has a powerful cyberteam already ripping apart Warren's life."

"Only if they have Detective Mannford's permission," she said.

A rumble erupted from his chest. "That's the legal avenue. But you're also our client, and that gives us rights on your behalf. So, no, not just with Detective Mannford's permission. We will share with him, don't you worry. The answers will be found now that this has happened. We're down to crunch time. And given the way this has all sped up, this weekend it may come crashing down."

Startled, she looked up at him. "You think the killer will come after me this weekend?"

"I do. I'm just hoping we recognize his face when he pops up in front of us."

Chapter 14

S HE WAS GETTING ready for bed when her phone rang. She answered to Levi asking, "Did you know Warren had a stepbrother?"

"No. Warren told me that he had no family left." She sat down on the bed as Tyson stood nearby in boxers. But even the sight of the gorgeous man in front of her couldn't still the fear snaking through her system at Levi's words. "Are we really thinking his stepbrother tried to kill him?"

"An original life insurance policy named his stepbrother as beneficiary. But that policy was canceled about six years ago, around the time Warren invested in the company."

"That makes sense. I imagine he was raising as much money as he could back then."

"He also sold off other assets in order to invest in the company. But he was close to bankruptcy when you came on board."

"I knew about that part," she said quietly. "I'm just not sure what brought on his wish to sell out right now."

"Still searching his history to answer those questions," Levi said. "His ex-wife got a decent divorce settlement, and the alimony was killing him, but they had agreed on a revised schedule, making his payments manageable. We'll keep digging. Do you know if he has any other family?"

"I didn't know about his stepbrother, so my answer

there is no."

"His stepbrother had a son with an ex-girlfriend. They broke up when the child was nine. He'd be eighteen now," Levi said.

She winced. "Change is hard for a boy that age."

"We haven't spoken with the mother, the ex-girlfriend, yet. She was trying to stop visitation rights. There were accusations of abuse."

"Which may or may not be true. In visitation cases, abuse is often used as leverage."

"I had another couple questions here for you," Levi said. "We're looking into his emails. Do you know a company called Viacom and another called Burning Edge?"

"The two are worlds apart. The first is great. It's a big video game company." She straightened. "What's his correspondence with them? He never told me about it." She couldn't stop the wave of excitement washing through her. Viacom was the big time.

"These were from a year ago, exploring a business arrangement. The most recent were with Burning Edge from a couple weeks ago."

"What did they say?" She frowned. "They aren't trustworthy, and I'd never deal with them."

"Let me dig deeper. I'll check in with you guys in the morning. Stay safe."

She put her phone on the night table and looked at Tyson. "Something must have happened to Warren in the last week. That's when this business-related disruption started."

"And the stalker geared up in the same time frame?"

She shook her head. "The stalker has been escalating for a couple weeks but clearly in this last week, yes."

Tyson nodded. He sat on the bed, propped against the

headboard and pulled his laptop onto his knees. "I'll do a bit of research into his last week. You need to get as much sleep as you can."

She curled up under the blankets beside him and whispered, "Not sure I'll ever sleep again. All I can see is Warren lying in the bathtub."

He stroked the strands of hair off her forehead. "I'm sorry you saw that."

"It doesn't matter," she whispered. "The reality is, right now we have to do whatever we can to make sure I'm not another victim. But also make sure you don't become one either. Or anybody else for that matter."

"We're on the same page there."

Just as she lay down, trying to let sleep slip through her mind, she asked, "Did you ever consider how Tracy would feel about us right now?"

Silence followed.

She shifted and saw his deep dark gaze, staring at her. "I believe she'd be happy," he said firmly. "She often told me that, if anything happened to her, I needed to go on without her and live a full life."

"And she told me that I needed to look after you," Kai said with a sad smile. "At the time I tried to be supportive, but you were not in great shape."

He snorted. "If that's what you call it, you're right there." He studied her for a long time.

And she knew instinctively when she saw the doubt enter, lurking in the background of his eyes, what he was thinking. She propped herself up on her elbow. "No."

He raised an eyebrow.

"No, that's not what this is. No, that's not why I'm in bed with you. I'm not looking after you. I am not listening to anything Tracy said. I was then, but I'm not now."

A ghost of a smile whispered across his lips, and he nodded. "Good, because I don't consider Tracy part of this. Tracy was my wife, and I loved her dearly. Then I lost her. I've mourned, and I've moved on. It just happens to be with her best friend. I think she would probably find it a blessing. I know I consider your presence in my life a blessing."

She relaxed at his words. "I loved Tracy, and I knew how much she cared for you. You two were right for each other. You were perfect together. I'm really glad you had the time you did with Tracy. She was so happy that last year."

Tyson brushed his thumb across Kai's lips, leaned over and kissed her. "Thank you for that. I'm so damn glad."

And in the next moment the laptop was off the bed, and once again they voraciously enjoyed each other.

Kai couldn't have been happier.

TYSON WOKE EARLY in the morning. Senses on full alert, he listened. But he heard nothing. He'd slept well, even if he was short on hours. He slipped free of the covers, careful not to disturb Kai, and walked through her small apartment.

He'd meant it when he had said he felt this weekend was crunch time. He just didn't know where the attack would come from or in what form the scorned lover or hired assassin would show up.

Finding nothing out of the ordinary, he returned to the bedroom and crept under the covers. But sleep wouldn't come.

He sat up and pulled out his laptop, quickly checking his emails, but there was no news from Levi, the detective or anybody else associated with either case. Then he checked the news to see if Warren's death had been leaked to the media. All appeared quiet.

In a way it was *too* quiet. He contemplated the little bit they knew. The stepbrother was an interesting angle. Back on his laptop, he quickly immersed himself in research on Warren and his family history. But all it did was take Tyson farther down the rabbit hole of the internet.

When Kai rolled over and propped herself up on her elbows to look at him, he smiled into those beautiful eyes. "Go back to sleep. I just couldn't sleep anymore."

Her cloudy gaze went from the laptop to him and back again. "Did you find anything?" She yawned, rolled over onto her side, pulling the blankets over her shoulders.

"No, not yet."

"We should check my employees."

He heard her half sleepy mumble and smiled. "We're on it."

She drifted off to sleep beside him, or at least he thought so. His phone buzzed, and he snatched it up to see a text from Ice.

Police are searching for Warren's stepbrother. He was military. Businessman in his own right. Sending photograph image two years ago.

The image, when it came, was a little grainy. He forwarded it to his email, then opened it on the laptop. He studied the face but didn't know it. It wasn't until he heard a sharp exclamation from Kai beside him that he realized she recognized him.

"Who's that?" she asked.

"Warren's stepbrother. The beneficiary of the life insurance policy that was canceled."

She shifted upright and leaned forward to look at him. "I

think I've see him in the office. Maybe just once," she said, her voice gentle. "The picture is kind of hazy."

"I'll see if I can find a better one."

He searched for images of the stepbrother and found five good ones. She checked them. "That looks like him. Maybe we can ask Tommy. The two of them were talking."

"Will do." He quickly sent Ice a text, adding a memo to himself. "We need to talk to Tommy but will wait until he wakes up."

Kai snorted. "And what time is it right now? It's a weekend. Tommy will be playing games all night long. He's probably just going to bed."

Tyson looked at her sharply. "Really?"

She nodded. "He usually crashes around six in the morning."

Tyson checked the clock on the nightstand. It was just after six. On a hunch, he dialed Tommy's number and listened to it ring. Worse case, he'd wake him up early in the morning on his day off and would have to listen to his tirade about that. Instead a relatively awake Tommy answered.

"It's Tyson. I'm here with Kai. Can you tell me anything about Warren's stepbrother?"

Hesitantly Tommy said, "I've met him a couple times. He has his own business."

"Has he ever been to the office?" Tyson asked, sensing the younger man was holding something back. Why?

"Yeah, a few times. Not much recently though. They had a fight."

"Any idea what the fight was about?" Tyson turned his gaze to Kai who was listening in on the conversation.

Tommy said, "No, not really. Something to do with money though. Seems like everybody's got money problems these days."

"How was Warren after the last meeting? Was he different?"

Tommy's voice turned curious but at the same time stiff. "I don't understand. Why all these questions? Do you think he's really got something to do with Kai's stalker?"

"No idea. That's what we're checking. I might have to call you back with some more questions." Before Tommy could ask any more of his own, Tyson hung up.

"That won't hold him for long," Kai said. "Warren's death will hit the media soon anyway, but we want to let the staff know before that time." She thought about it and sat up. "I feel like I should tell Tommy myself."

"Let me check with Ice and see if we have permission yet."

He texted Ice and got a response back within seconds. "She said, yes. Media has already got a hold of it. It will be today's headlines."

Chapter 15

KAI GRABBED HER phone and called Tommy. She put it on Speaker so Tyson could hear. She didn't get a chance to even say hi before Tommy asked, "What the hell's going on?"

Her voice tired, she said, "Have you seen the headlines?"

"Why would I listen to the news? You and I both know most of it is garbage."

"Well, today will be some upsetting garbage. Warren is dead."

Tommy sucked in his breath in shocked silence.

"There's no easy way to break it to you. I'm sorry for the call so early in the morning. We went by his place last night to talk to him." She rubbed a hand across her forehead. "We found him dead in his apartment."

"What? ... How did he die?"

"We're waiting on the autopsy results. We're not sure if he committed suicide or if he was murdered, but it was made to look like he committed suicide."

"What!" Tommy exclaimed. "There's no way he would've committed suicide."

"Why is that?" Tyson asked.

"Because he was heading off on a vacation."

"You knew about his flight out?" Kai asked sharply.

"I don't know about a flight, but he said he was leaving

next weekend, and he was excited about an upcoming holiday. He was really closemouthed about it. I figured he had some hot chick stashed somewhere who he didn't want to share. You know what it's like at the office," Tommy admitted. "I figured he was just keeping her all to himself."

"Well, he was certainly taking a flight over the weekend," Kai said quietly. "Unfortunately it was a one-way ticket to Thailand."

"Thailand?" Tommy said, impressed. "Wow, really?" There was a long pause before he said, "Wait a minute. Did you say a one-way ticket?"

"Yeah. Warren was leaving next weekend. And he wasn't planning on coming back."

Through the silence on the phone she could almost hear Tommy's heartbeat. She realized just how much Tommy had looked up to Warren. "You knew Warren really well, didn't you?"

Tommy's voice was strangled when he said, "Yes. At least I thought so."

"I don't think he was thinking straight at the end, if that helps."

"He was thinking straight enough to make decisions like that though, wasn't he?" There was unmistakable bitterness in Tommy's tone.

She winced. "Yes, as much as I hate to think about that. ... Maybe he just wanted time to figure out his next step. It's hard to walk away from everyone." She was trying to stay positive for Tommy's sake. He was only eighteen. And, although he was a genius in so many ways, he lacked a lot of stability in his relationships, and this was just, yet again, another ugly spot in his life.

"He was my uncle, you know? Or maybe step-uncle is a

better term. I don't know. His stepbrother is my father by blood but not in any other way. In truth I can't stand him or the way he operates," Tommy said stiffly. "When in the same room we don't even acknowledge each other."

She sat upright, the shock almost visceral. "Really? You're related? Oh, I'm so sorry, Tommy. I didn't know." Tyson laid his hand on her thigh, but she could feel the tears gathering in the back of her eyes. "That makes it so much worse."

"Yeah, it does, doesn't it?" Tommy said. "My mother was Warren's stepbrother's girlfriend for a long time. So the connection wasn't by blood or marriage. And when my parents split up, my father had nothing to do with her or me. Warren, at the time, got involved and probably paid my mother off. I don't know why. Maybe he felt responsible for his useless stepbrother." Tommy's tone of voice slowed, his emotions ragged. "My mother was no winner either. She was looking for money back then and many times since. It's quite possible Warren helped her out over time as he stayed in touch all those years. When he offered me a job, I accepted. I can do the work, but I don't get along so well with people." His voice was low. "As you well know."

"I never had a problem with you, Tommy. And our everyday experiences should help our relationships get easier, but sometimes we lose the people we love without any warning."

"Isn't that the truth?" His voice broke, and he hung up.

She'd heard the sob in his throat—knew he would have a really tough time dealing with Warren's death. She leaned back down and said, "Christ, I feel bad now. Did the police know?"

"It's quite possible they didn't," Tyson said. "I just told

Levi and Ice to track down Tommy's mother and see what they can find out."

"It's all so confusing."

"It will all be untwisted soon."

"And then I have to wonder who inherits," she said. "Does Warren have a will, and is Tommy in it?"

"YOU SUSPECT TOMMY?" Tyson asked, his voice neutral.

She shook her head. "No, I don't. That took a little too much organization for him. Tommy might hit out in a rage, but I can't see him systematically slicing Warren's wrists. Not to mention the fact he faints at the sight of blood."

Tyson raised an eyebrow.

"I cut myself with the coffeepot the first week working there. I felt pretty stupid, but I saw Tommy's face, and he almost passed out. I had to force him to sit down, his head between his knees, while I cleaned up the mess."

"And you don't think he was faking it?"

"No, he wasn't faking it. He almost passed out." She threw back the covers and grabbed up her robe. As she put it on she said, "I certainly can't sleep now."

She walked to the kitchen and made coffee. While waiting for the brew to drip, she stared out the kitchen window. Somehow it was just so much worse knowing Tommy had been related to Warren. The police should have notified Tommy of his loss. Now the police would be knocking on his door, asking questions he wouldn't have any answers for.

As she poured the coffee, she wondered about the other employees. They all seemed quite chummy. She pulled out her phone and sent Tommy a text. **Did anyone else at the company know you were related to Warren?**

The answer came back fast. **Larry did. We've been friends for years. As for the others, no idea. It was never discussed.**

Thanks. Do you know if Warren has any other family?

Just his stepbrother. Warren didn't have any children of his own.

"Right," she said aloud. She walked to the bedroom to stand in the doorway. "Tommy doesn't think anybody else in the company is related to Warren, but they haven't discussed it. He says Warren only had the stepbrother that he knew about."

Tyson didn't look up from his laptop, but he answered, "That's what I'm finding too. We need to contact Warren's lawyer to find out more."

TYSON'S PHONE RANG. He picked it up and answered, "Levi, what's up?"

"Detective Mannford contacted Warren's lawyer, and there was a partner life insurance policy for the business. With Warren's death, Kai now owns the business one hundred percent. Warren did have a will. Kai's not in it. Tommy is. But Tommy does not inherit any of the company."

"Okay, that makes sense. She just spoke to Tommy, not realizing they were related, and broke Warren's death to Tommy. He's pretty devastated about it."

"Yes, Warren apparently helped Tommy out over the last decade. Warren's stepbrother was contacted by the police to let him know about his brother's death. He's not in the will. They're looking for any life insurance policy or other motive for the stepbrother to kill Warren but haven't found anything. The stepbrother owns Burning Edge. So we're looking into that angle. But we don't have any answers yet."

Interesting that Burning Edge was the stepbrother's company. Tyson's mind immediately tried to work the angles and fit that information into the bits he already knew. "Does Warren have other assets?"

"The apartment he lived in. But it was due to close the day after he was murdered. Not sure what happens to that now. That's up to the lawyers to sort out."

Tyson nodded. "Right. So no reason you know of for killing Warren. It doesn't make any sense."

"Unless it has to do with the stepbrother's connection."

"In what way?"

"For instance, if the stepbrother thought his company was getting exclusive rights to the VR system. He says Warren gave him a signed contract."

"Yet Kai knows nothing about it and certainly didn't sign that contract."

"Maybe Warren tried to pull a fast one, like sell the software to his stepbrother's company for some traveling cash. Warren must have known he would be in trouble as soon as Kai found out, so he decided to get out of it."

"That's possible. But Burning Edge doesn't have a chance of enforcing the contract if it's not transferred from both owners. So we need a signed original of that document to know for sure. Warren's lawyer should have a copy. He handled the business side of things."

"I'll call him." Levi hung up.

Tyson looked up as Kai walked in with a cup of coffee. He quickly shared the details learned from Levi's phone call.

She sat down on the bed. "We never discussed selling of

the VR program to Burning Edge. Warren knew how I felt about that particular company. I thought he felt the same. Burning Edge operates on the shady side. Never once did Warren mention it was his stepbrother's company." She frowned. Then added slowly, "*Why was that?* Obviously Warren probably didn't want anyone to know. And of course he knew how poor a reputation Burning Edge had. Tommy would have known as well."

"Whether he was ashamed of his father or just angry still over him being an absentee father, I imagine Burning Edge was something Tommy would *not* want brought up over and over."

"Right. There's no way any deal prior to my arrival would've been made because we didn't have this progress on the VR system yet, so, if the contract was made afterward, that would mean Warren was trying to sneak something over on me."

"Why would he do that?"

"No idea. We have to talk to the lawyers. That'll tell us what contracts there are and whether they are legal and binding." She ran her hand over her face, stopping to rub her tired eyes. "This is such a nightmare."

"Or it could be perfect. On his death, his interest in the company reverts to you a hundred percent."

"I signed something like that too." She brightened. "Do you know that for sure?"

"Sure as I can be without seeing the paperwork. And of course that means, as far as the police are concerned, you move to suspect number one."

"I always was suspect number one," she said drily. "But I also have you as an alibi. And, if Tommy is inheriting Warren's house and his bank accounts and anything else …"

"I know he inherits a lot. I don't know if he inherits everything."

She nodded. "That makes him suspect number two."

"Exactly."

"With no other family but Tommy, I guess the funeral arrangements fall to him and Warren's stepbrother."

"Yes." Tyson thought about Tommy with his lime green pants and purple tie. "I can't really imagine Tommy setting up funeral arrangements."

Kai gave Tyson a sad smile. "I like that about him. He is innocent in so many ways. I'm really hoping this doesn't change that. But of course losing a mentor and family member you care about, well, everything changes." She looked at Tyson. "How can it not?"

He focused on his keyboard because of course she was right. Hadn't it changed for him? "Have I changed that much?"

She stopped on her way to the bathroom, her eyebrows raised. "I wasn't thinking of you when I said that," she said. "In a way, I was thinking of me."

It was his turn to be surprised. "In what way?"

She gave a crooked smile. "I'm more me. Back then when I was with her, I was an extension of Tracy. When I was alone, I felt like I wasn't quite complete. The last two years was all about learning who I was. Doing things because I wanted to and not because she wanted to. I was learning the foods I like again versus the food she wanted. She was a force of nature, and I was a happy tree to bow in the wind. But, when I lost her, my energy wasn't directed in one way or another." She laughed a bit. "I had to figure out who I was, what direction I wanted to go. Just as Tommy will have to do."

She walked into the bathroom, closing the door gently behind her. He stared at the door in wonder because Tracy had, indeed, been a force of nature. She'd been very good at coercing people into doing what she wanted them to do. Always with a gentle smile, but no doubt she had been a dominant force directing her world and his. He hadn't been thinking about getting married, but, as long as she wanted to, he was good with it. He hadn't been delirious about having a family, but, before he knew it, it was already happening. Even the house they bought together had been because she had adored it. When she was happy, he was happy.

For the first time he understood Kai's earlier question about whether his relationship with Tracy would have lasted. Would his marriage have gone the distance? Would they have survived ten or even twenty years together? He'd still like to think so. But to do so, he knew there would've been a lot of compromise on his part.

At the time he'd been totally okay with that. Now maybe he was a little more like Kai, in that he'd learned a lot. As if that year with Tracy, working and smiling and laughing, had made his world brighter and so full of joy. Then, when it emptied out, he had reverted to the same quiet person he'd been before.

As he leaned against the headboard, he had to wonder if that was a bad thing.

Not that he was quiet because he was sad, and it wasn't that he was depressed. He was just naturally reserved. It'd been exhausting being around Tracy. But he'd never wanted to let her down, never wanted her to look at him with disappointment. He'd have done anything and everything he could to keep the sunshine on her face. Going forward he would've adapted.

But it was so strange now to realize just how different life was without her. And yet, it was not that it was bad. In fact, maybe for the first time, he realized it would really be okay.

Chapter 16

A FTER COFFEE KAI looked at him and said, "What do you want to do now?"

He closed the laptop, placed it off to the side and turned to look at her. "It's Saturday. What would you like to do?"

"I think we should return to the office, go through Warren's computer, find out if there's anything we should know about."

"I have no problem with that. You should probably stop by the lawyer's too, if he's willing to see us on a Saturday."

"Will the detective give us an update?"

"Hard to say. I can call him later and see."

"Okay, breakfast first? If you're hankering for pancakes."

He grinned. "I've always got room for pancakes."

They showered and dressed quickly. He drove to the restaurant and sat down with yet more coffee.

"You think there is any chance the autopsy will be done today?" Kai asked.

"I doubt it, but considering it's now a murder investigation, I can't say for sure."

They ordered breakfast. When they were almost done, Tyson got a phone call from Ice. "Good morning to you too." Tyson smiled, put the phone on Speaker and laid it on the table. "You're on speakerphone, Ice. Go ahead."

"The coroner is doing the autopsy this week. We'll

hopefully get a full report by Friday. It will give us something solid to go on. Her tone was such that Kai knew it was more worry about them than thinking they were taking too many chances. "We have several investigations ongoing here but answers on some fronts take time. I don't need to warn you guys about being careful."

Kai chuckled. "I'm not planning on doing anything major. Right now we're having pancakes."

"Lucky for you guys. I missed breakfast. However, Alfred's making me something right now."

"Lucky you." Kai laughed. "I'd take Alfred's breakfast over restaurant food any day." She caught Tyson's strange look but ignored it.

"We're heading into the office afterward," Tyson said. "We want to check Warren's computer, particularly if this is a murder investigation. The police are likely to come and take everything."

"That's not a bad idea. Make sure you go through any physical files and whatever else might be pertinent."

The longer she sat there, the more Kai worried the police would do just that before they had a chance to look for themselves. She faced Tyson and said, "I sense a sudden urgency to go."

He got up to pay the bill. By the time he was done, Kai waited impatiently at the front door. As he hopped into the vehicle, he asked, "Any reason in particular?"

She shrugged. "I don't know how long before the autopsy is completed. Once it's declared a murder investigation, I'm afraid the company will shut down for a while."

He drove straight to the business and pulled into the parking lot. She was surprised to see several vehicles there. "Why is anybody here? We're closed today."

"Let's go find out."

"Has Ice said if anything unusual has shown up on any of the security cameras we installed?"

"No, and that means no one has. She won't relax on this one."

When she let them into the office, they found Tommy and Larry sitting off to the side. Tommy looked a little worse for wear. When he saw her, he walked over, his arms open wide. She gave him a hug and held him. For all his brain-power, he was still just a big teenager.

"I'm so sorry, Tommy."

He sniffled and stepped back. "Still can't believe it."

"I know. The autopsy is this week." She walked over to Warren's office door and tried to open it, but it was locked. She turned toward Tommy. "Did you lock it?"

Tommy shook his head. "I figured you did. I came in to make sure everything was secure. I started to think about the police shutting us down. I tried getting into his office but couldn't."

"How long have you been here?" she asked, suspicion still driving her instincts forward. She glanced at Larry. "And you?"

"We came in together. Just got in about ten minutes before you," Tommy said.

When she turned back to Warren's office, the door was open. Tyson gave her a bland look. She walked in, headed to the back of Warren's desk and turned on the computer. His laptop was still here. She frowned. She took hers home every night. Then again how many did he have? She only had one. "Was there a laptop in Warren's apartment?" she asked Tyson.

He shook his head. "No, there wasn't. Were you expecting one to be here?"

She frowned. "I knew he had one. I just wondered if he had two."

"I take my laptop back and forth," Tommy said from the doorway. "Warren has two laptops, I think. But one was so old it almost wasn't workable anymore. I think it's in the bottom drawer of the filing cabinet."

"Has anybody touched the servers or accessed the computer in the last twenty-four hours?" she asked, walking over to check the filing cabinet. Sure enough a laptop was there.

Tommy looked at her in surprise and frowned and then horror hit his expression, and he bolted to his desk.

Her stomach sank as she said, "I guess we'll find out in a few minutes." She sat down and opened Warren's desk drawers.

Larry walked over. "Should you be doing that?"

"Yes, I should. Seeing that I'm the remaining partner in the business, I need to know what the hell's going on." She didn't watch his face, only got an odd look from him when she glanced up. "That bothers you?"

"Tommy might be the other partner now."

She looked at Larry for a long moment, realizing nobody really knew about the legal side of this yet. And how many of the employees knew about Tommy and Warren's relationship? "That might be. But if you think I'd do anything to destroy the business, you're wrong. I need to know what's going on, and that means going through Warren's desk. Regardless of who gets Warren's shares, I'm still the majority shareholder."

Larry shrugged, stepping back slightly. She watched him as he glanced over at Tyson. But Larry's face was hard, his glance steady on the doorway.

"Did that seem odd to you?" she asked in a low enough tone so Larry couldn't hear them.

"Oh, yeah. I'll contact Ice and see if she ever got a full report on him."

She nodded. "Do that."

She went through all of Warren's desk. In the file drawer he had several matching folders like the ones she kept her contracts in. However, also in the drawer was a sealed black leather case. She pulled it out, opened it up and inside found the Burning Edge material. While Tyson went over the laptop, she pulled out the paperwork and took a closer look. It included copies of emails, contract details on the product and more that she handed over to Levi for testing. "Well, isn't this interesting?"

"What did you find?"

"The Burning Edge folder. And what appears to be a contract."

"So he was doing this without your permission?" He studied her carefully. "I'm sorry."

"Me too. I wonder if I ever knew him." She started to pore over the contract, not liking the terms, not liking anything about it. If he'd already made a deal with them, albeit without her permission, why was it he'd been okay with her taking the VR system to Levi as a prototype? According to the contract before her, Burning Edge would have had exclusive rights to develop and market the VR system.

When she got to the signing partners' signatures, she found a spot for hers, but no signature was there. And she was pretty damn sure that made the contract illegal.

She'd have to read the contract and see what the details were but later, much later. Even after that she'd have to run it by her attorney. She folded it up, put it away and continued looking in the rest of Warren's desk drawers. Leaving the black leather case on the desk, she walked over to the filing cabinet and went through it. She'd been through these files many times before as these were the only hard copies of the company's files. Behind all the files was a strong box. She drew that out. "And this is interesting too."

Tyson looked up, his gaze lighting when he saw the box in her hand. "Put it down here. If it's locked, I'll pop it open for you."

She put it on the desk, and of course it was locked. She looked in the top drawer, finding a small jewelry box where Warren kept the key. Inside was cash. A lot of cash. Hearing footsteps outside, she quickly closed it and put it on her lap so nobody walking in could see it.

Tommy came in. "It doesn't appear anything's been touched on the servers."

The relief in his voice made her realize just how much Tommy had invested in this company as well.

"Good. Now can you check if anybody used Warren's log-in to gain access, and, if they did, what files they looked at?"

Tommy nodded. As he turned away, his gaze landed on the black case. "Oh, that's Warren's. I saw him with that earlier."

She looked up, patted the black leather case and said, "You mean this?"

Tommy nodded.

"Inside is a contract he signed with Burning Edge for exclusive development and marketing rights on our VR system."

"What?" Tommy looked shell-shocked. "How could he

do that? They have a horrible reputation. I know he's my father with a shitty company, but … I had no idea he was such an asshole."

"Yeah, that could be why Warren's dead. Warren signed a contract—without my signature—to give Burning Edge the VR system." Inside her stomach hurt. She needed to contact her lawyer on that one. Why would Warren do that? Fast cash? Or did his stepbrother have something to hold over Warren's head as leverage? It would have to be something major …

Tommy stared at her in horror. "Please tell me that contract's not legal."

"I'm not sure yet. But I sure as hell didn't sign this contract. The lawyers will have to hammer it out. And then they'll have to hammer out Burning Edge, but I'm hoping to confirm the contract is not binding."

"You know what we have going here is huge, right?" His earnest expression showed even through his mop of hair covered most of his face. "We can do so much better than that nightmare company."

"And that's why I don't understand why Warren did it." She shook her head. "It doesn't make any sense. Maybe he knew it wasn't legal. Maybe he did it to get them off his back, and when they found out …" She let her voice trail off.

Tommy winced. "Oh, I can see that. Burning Edge has an ugly rep."

"How good are your hacking skills?" Tyson asked him.

Tommy gave him an innocent baby-blue-eyed look. "Hacking is illegal."

"And we all know about your history. It looks like Warren has his laptop security coded. Any idea how to get into it?"

"Man, why would he do that? This is his office unit," Tommy said.

"Exactly. Which is why we need to get into this computer. We need to know if somebody used his log-in information. How good is your security here?"

"The best," Tommy said. "It's what I do."

"You mean, it's what you used to do," Kai said with a chuckle. "Now you're only involved with legal activities."

"One has to learn how to break the bank in order to understand how to stop others from doing the same thing," Tommy said absentmindedly. His gaze focused on the laptop. "I'll use password breaking software for this. It won't take too long. Then I should be able to get in through the network. But that won't allow me into his personal emails. He has a company email we can access without any trouble. But his personal emails are a different story." He picked up Warren's office computer. "You want me to do this now?"

"Yes. Before the police show up with a warrant and take anything they want."

Tommy looked at Kai in horror and raced out the door.

Tyson stood and whispered, "I'll watch him. We need everything on that laptop."

"Go do that. We have to figure out why Warren has so much cash sitting at his desk."

Tyson gave her a hard look as he walked out. "Because he needed it to run."

He closed the door behind him, giving her a chance to open up the strongbox again and take a serious look at the money. Over thirty thousand in cash sat in the box. As she stared out the window, she had to wonder. "Warren, did you take a bribe? And, when they realized the contract wouldn't stand up in court, did they come after you? Thirty thousand wasn't worth killing you over."

She closed the box and placed it inside her bag. It was a damn tight fit, but no way would she leave that kind of money here. Not when the guys all had access to it. She didn't know how this worked. Did she have the rights to it? Yet another question for the lawyers.

TYSON FOLLOWED TOMMY out to the main office where he sat down in front of a hard drive connected to his main computer, then connected it to the laptop. Instantly, Tyson saw the password cracking program start working on the laptop. He smiled to himself. "How often do you get to use that program?"

Tommy gave him a sheepish grin. "Not enough, that's for sure."

Larry sat down at his own desk, but he made no attempt to work. He put his feet up and watched Tommy.

"You know anything about what Warren was doing?" Tyson asked him.

Larry shrugged. "Nope, I sure don't."

His tone of voice was less than caring. Tommy didn't seem to notice. Tyson wondered at the relationship between Tommy and Larry who appeared to be eight to ten years older. Tommy was just young enough and stupid-smart enough to be taken in by somebody. He was geekwise, not worldwise. Tyson had seen it happen time and time again.

He decided to sit back and just watch the two of them. While he kept up via texts in the ongoing conversation with the detective about details and with Levi forwarding information, Tyson quietly took pictures of Larry and Tommy.

He knew Ice could pick up on body language in a

spooky way. Even via photos. Merk and Rhodes were really good at that too. But both of them were off on jobs. Stone could read others too yet tended to be home more now. It wasn't that his leg kept him from doing whatever he needed to do, but more that his security-related skills were needed at the compound. He was doing a big overhaul on the security system to encompass all the new apartments being remodeled.

While Tyson took care of his own business and kept watching the two young men in front of him, Tyson also watched as Tommy worked his way through the system to see if Warren had logged in within the last twenty-four hours.

"He logged out yesterday afternoon before he stormed out of here," Tommy said quietly. "He didn't log in again."

"So that's good."

"Why's that good?" Larry challenged Tyson. "I don't understand what you have to do with any of us."

Tyson ignored him. He wanted to see just how aggressive the young man would get.

Tommy looked at Larry who sat beside Tyson, then switched his gaze back. "Do you have any right to know this stuff?"

Tyson nodded. "Yes, I do."

The relief on Tommy's face made Tyson realize just how young Tommy really was.

"So you say. You're nothing but her latest lay," Larry sneered.

Tyson straightened ever-so-slightly. Larry's feet hit the floor, and he backed up. Tyson measured the younger man with cold eyes. "Who are you talking about right now?"

His voice was so soft, so deadly, it sent Tommy into a

spiel. "He didn't mean it. He talks about all women that way."

"He will never talk about one woman again like that." Tyson pinned Larry in place with his gaze. "Do you understand?"

Larry tried to puff up his chest but caved in quickly. "Yeah, I understand." His voice was solid but his demeanor was cowed.

Tyson studied him for a long moment. "It might be time to look for another job."

Both young men stood in front of him. "There is no reason for that," Tommy said anxiously. "Larry's really good at what he does."

Tyson turned his head sideways, looking at Tommy. "What exactly does Larry do here?"

Larry frowned and looked at Tommy. "I do all kinds of stuff."

Tommy nodded, puzzled. "Why?"

"Because nobody who appreciates their job and understands just what a delicate balance they're in right now would talk about their boss like he just did," Tyson said.

"She doesn't have anything to do with the business. This was Warren's company. Warren explained it all to me," Larry said, finding his bravado again.

At that both Tommy and Tyson looked at him. "What do you mean, Larry?" Tommy asked.

Larry looked at Tommy and scoffed. "Hey, you know how it goes. She brought in a little bit of money, and she acts like she owns the place. Now look at him. He's dead, and I bet she killed him."

Tommy shook his head. "No way. That's not how it was."

"Warren told me how she didn't pay full price for everything, that she barely gave enough to bail him out of trouble. Her presence here was temporary, as part of the contract that he could buy the shares back as soon as he raised the money." Larry went back to reclining in his chair, his feet up on the desk. "She killed him. I don't know why the hell anybody would be looking any further than her. It should be your company, Tommy. Everybody knows that."

Tommy shook his head. "No, that's not true. This was Mark and Warren's company first. I came on soon after so I was there almost from the beginning. But I was just a kid then so not official in any way."

"Everything should come to you. But what do you want to bet that bitch there will find a way to make sure you don't get it?"

Tyson eyed Larry steadily, listened quietly, wondering just what Larry's role in all of this was.

Tommy sat down. "I'd rather have my uncle than his company. Besides, Kai told the truth. She has a controlling interest in the company, not Warren."

Larry shoved his chin out. "No way."

Tommy nodded. "I asked the lawyer yesterday after they argued."

Tyson filed that away. Interesting Tommy had the smarts to do that.

Larry stared at his friend in shock. "No way! That's wrong. I know she was lying. Warren warned me how she would spread lies like that. And she did when we talked about it before. No way Warren would give up controlling interest of the company. Who are you going to believe? Her or our boss?"

Of course Larry had never thought of Kai as his boss.

Warren had been here first. She was nothing but an upstart to the both of them. Too bad. Kai deserved better.

"He had no choice in it," Tommy said. "He was in bankruptcy. She bailed him out too, and that meant all our jobs. And I appreciate that she did. I don't know that I would fit into too many other places. This is the best job for me. When Uncle Warren brought me on, I was delighted. You know what I'm like when I get around strangers or people who don't know who I am. I'm awkward. I just don't function well."

Larry stared at him in horror, then glanced at the closed door. "You mean she actually owns the company?"

Tommy nodded. "Yeah, she has since Mark died."

Tyson watched Larry's face as a gray cast suddenly overtook his features. That this was news was one thing. That it was incredibly bad news was a whole different story.

"Now that Warren's dead, it should be yours. Warren would have a will. Surely he left his half to you."

"I don't think it works that way when it comes to businesses."

"But he had you, Tommy. You're his nephew. You might not see that bond as blood but he viewed you as family. He said you inherited everything—remember that?"

Tommy looked at Larry. "He was joking. I'm pretty sure it was part of the business agreement. If she died, he got the company. If he died, she got the company."

"No, that can't be."

"Why not, Larry?" Tyson asked. "Because then you killed Warren for nothing?"

Fear stabbed the man's eyes. He shook his head rapidly. "No, no, no, no. That can't be. The company is yours, Tommy. You'll just have to figure it out. This guy's full of shit." He waved at Tyson. "You don't belong here. It's that bitch you're with."

Tyson took a step toward him. Larry jackrabbited out of his chair and raced backward. "Don't let him hurt me, Tommy."

Tommy stood, his tall lanky form a beanpole between the two men. "What Tyson said," Tommy asked Larry, "was he right?"

"No, of course he wasn't right. I never hurt anyone."

"Unless hurting Warren would have helped you, Tommy, and then Larry by default. You've been friends for a long time, haven't you?" Tyson asked lightly, his mind suddenly seeing how this would work.

Larry nodded. "We've been friends since forever, haven't we, Tommy?"

"Yes, we have," Tommy said. "He's like an older brother to me." Yet, Tommy stared at Larry as if he'd never seen him before.

Tyson understood why. When one finally understood what people were capable of, it was often a shock. "What did you do when you found out Warren was leaving?" Tyson asked Larry. "That he was running away, out of the country, and leaving everything to collapse behind him?" Tyson heard the door to Warren's office open quietly. He realized Kai must've heard or seen something to make her aware of what was going on out here.

"I went to his apartment, talked to him. I asked him if he was leaving. If he realized the company would collapse if he left. He denied it. He denied he was leaving.

"He had a lot of cash with him. It was a down payment on a contract. But he needed it to start his new life." Larry shook his head in bewilderment. "He was going to leave

Tommy and me, and she couldn't possibly keep the company going. I knew it would go under. Warren explained to me how she didn't have any power to do anything. She would lose her job, not that I cared about her, but Tommy and I'd been here for a long time. This was our company too."

"You killed Warren, didn't you, Larry?" Tyson asked quietly. He glanced down at his phone to make sure it was recording the video as it played out.

"But I didn't mean to. I didn't mean to hurt him. We fought, and he fell. I guess I hit him a bit too hard. I don't know if it was my punch that made him hit the bathroom counter as he went down. I didn't mean to hurt him."

"So why did you put him in the bathtub and cut his wrists?" Kai asked quietly from the doorway. "And then go back and clean up the blood. Why not call for an ambulance and get him the help he needed?"

Larry's face turned to fury. "Because he was still leaving us. As soon as he got better again, he would still leave us." He shrugged. "I put the money I found at his place back in the strongbox in the office. That's where he took it from. It's where it belonged. The company is Tommy's. I'd never steal from him."

"You did steal from him. You stole his family, his mentor—the man who helped pay for Tommy's education through the years, the man who gave Tommy holidays and helped him when his mother couldn't."

"No! You see? It was an accident."

"It was an accident," Tyson said, "until you cut Warren's wrists and let him bleed out."

"And then it became murder." Kai's voice was soft, gentle. But she wasn't looking at Larry. She was studying Tommy. The young kid had gone from fear to anger, and now he looked like he was ready to burst into tears. She walked closer and put her hand on his shoulder. "Sit down, Tommy."

He collapsed into his chair as he stared at Larry. "Please tell me that you didn't kill Uncle Warren."

Larry held out his hands. "I didn't mean to, Tommy. And then I panicked. I didn't know what else to do. He wasn't bleeding, but he was breathing. He was still alive when I put him in the bathtub."

"He was still alive when you cut his wrists? In other words, if you'd called the ambulance, you might have saved him?" Kai asked. "Instead, now it's murder. And you were the stalker, weren't you? You're the one driving me crazy? The one texting me, telling me to make a decision? Inputting fake names into my cell phone? Following me, stealing my underwear? Tracking me?"

Larry shrugged. "Yeah, but I did it at Warren's request."

Chapter 17

"**W**ITH WARREN'S PERMISSION?" Kai asked in shock. "Yeah, he didn't want you around. I figured that, if I made life really difficult for you, then you'd run away."

"So why did he panic and try to run?" Tommy asked, his voice hard.

"Because stalking and fraud carry some severe sentences. And I think he understood he was about to get found out," Tyson said.

Tommy looked at Tyson in surprise. "What are you talking about?"

"When I brought in Legendary Security to investigate the stalker, we started looking at everyone in this company," Kai said. "And Warren panicked. He'd hired Larry to terrorize me by making me think I had a stalker." She shrugged. "It was a shitty thing to do but hardly worth throwing his life away for."

"It wasn't just that," Tyson said in a low tone.

She narrowed her gaze at him, seeing the signs of impending bad news in his careful look. "What did you find out?"

Tyson reached out a hand for Kai. "Mark. His death wasn't an accident."

Kai gasped in horror. "Please no," she cried out. "Mark

was a good man. He was my friend."

"Sorry, Kai, but the police have opened an investigation into his death. Mark left a notepad on his desk where he'd been working through some issues. His sister contacted the police when she read them. Mark was concerned as Warren was really angry when Mark contacted you. Even though Warren needed the money, he didn't want to sell enough shares to bail out the company, essentially transferring one-third ownership out of his hands. He'd threatened Mark several times."

Kai, tears in her eyes, said, "By killing Mark, Warren thought he'd inherit Mark's shares. Which, added to his own, gave him a controlling interest. And, by selling off part to me, he'd get out of the financial hell he'd gotten into, and this way he wouldn't lose the company. Only Mark lay on his death bed for several days, and, in the meantime, our paperwork was completed, making me a shareholder and, with the way the contract was written between them, Mark now had a choice to leave the shares to me instead of Warren." She shook her head. "And I had no idea. Poor Mark."

"Poor Mark, indeed."

"Jesus, Mark was awesome. That sucks," Tommy whispered. "Was anything about Uncle Warren like I thought it was?"

"Don't think that," Larry said. "Warren wasn't a bad man. He was desperate."

Tommy turned to look at Larry. "How can you say that? He killed his partner. He helped you terrorize Kai. Then he tried selling one of our products to one of the worst companies possible." He shook head. "He was about to run and leave the company hanging."

"He should have killed Kai. Then he'd have had the money and all the stock in the company," Larry cried out.

"And looked guilty as hell too," Tyson said quietly. "That would have triggered an investigation he couldn't afford."

"No way. He'd have done it so no one knew. Like he killed Mark."

"I would have investigated," Tyson said, his voice hard and cold. "I'd have turned every stone to make sure I got the answers I needed. Then I'd have made damn sure he paid."

"Which is why Warren panicked when I brought in Legendary," Kai said quietly. "Warren knew his chances of escaping punishment were damn small."

"So he decided to sell his place and run." Tommy turned to stare at his uncle's office. "I feel like I never knew him at all."

"Don't worry, Tommy," Tyson said. "With Warren's death, we'll track down all related bank accounts, looking for any hidden deals."

"You won't honor the contract? Was that hush money Larry brought back? A prepayment or maybe a bribe?" Tommy asked, surprise and hope in his voice. "Can we get out of it?"

"I never signed the contract," Kai said. "Warren had no right to sell or make an agreement without my signature." She hesitated. "As for the money I don't know. I doubt Burning Edge will say it was from them. A deposit wasn't mentioned in any of the paperwork."

"But can Burning Edge still enforce the contract?"

She shrugged. "Not sure how they can, not when I have controlling interest in the company, and Warren was only a partner." She smiled at Tommy. "We'll sort it out."

"I don't want any contract with them."

She nodded. "I'm in full agreement. But we have a bit of a mess we need to sort out now."

"What does that mean?"

"It means, we're not taking anything to market for at least another six months, until this thing blows over," she said calmly. "We may end up with some legal issues we have to figure out first, but then we will rebuild bigger and better. And, when we talk about gaming companies, we're not going with Burning Edge. An awful lot of bigger, better companies are out there, like Viacom."

"Absolutely. So you're keeping the company going?" Tommy asked hopefully.

She smiled. "With your skills, I'm sure we can take the company far."

Larry shouted. "It should be *his* company."

Tommy shook his head. "I don't know anything about business. I just want to do what I do."

"And that's why you do what you do, and that's why I do what I do," Kai said with a smile. "Obviously I will need to hire some new staff." She looked pointedly at Larry. "You do realize you've ruined your future and your life as a whole?"

He turned to look at his friend. "Tommy, you'll get me out of this, right?" He inched toward the front door. "I did all this for you."

Tommy looked at him. "Larry, you've been like a brother to me, but, dude, when you mess up, you mess up big."

Larry's face twisted in anger. "After all I did so you'd get your damn company? You're the genius behind the company. It should be yours. I know for a fact you could run it."

"How would you know that?" Tyson asked quietly.

"Because I talked to Warren about it. He and I were good friends, and I was one of the few who knew about his and Tommy's relationship. He assured me that Tommy got everything." He glared at Kai. "And that means *everything.*"

She shook her head. "And how is it that you can still believe Warren after all he did? Tommy will likely inherit something, but I think the company is now mine, one hundred percent."

Larry's face filled with such rage that he was probably contemplating attacking her. Tyson had yet to move. She wanted Larry to try something so she could beat the crap out of him. But of course, cowardly to the end, he turned and raced for the front door. He threw it open, and, as he headed out, several policemen surrounded him.

"No, no, no, no. You can't do this. Tommy, help me." He screamed all the way down the hall, all the way down the stairs.

Finally his screams couldn't be heard anymore. Kai turned her attention to Tommy, who sat hunched over, tears in his eyes.

She glanced at Tyson and then gave Tommy a big hug. "This is probably the worst day of your life. However, it'll get better after this."

He shook his head. "How can it ever be good again?"

"Don't let your uncle's murder be the end of you. Make something of your work. Prove it can be done without lying and cheating," Tyson said quietly. He motioned to the detective at the door.

"Unfortunately I have a lot of questions for you for the next few hours."

"What about his stepbrother—my father—is he in trouble too?" Tommy asked.

Detective Mannford walked toward them and answered, "Yes, he is. But more for fraud. I don't believe he had anything to do with your uncle's murder. And I don't think he had anything to do with the stalking issues."

"No, just for whatever Burning Edge was up to," Kai said.

Several hours later they took Tommy home to his place. At the end of the police questioning, he'd been pretty broken up. Detective Mannford had offered to give Tommy a ride, but he'd looked at Kai, so she took him home.

When they dropped him off, making sure he had a couple friends to stay with him, she walked back out with Tyson and said, "So does that mean you're heading home to your place now?"

"Where is my place?" he asked. "The compound is about forty minutes from here. Currently I have been living with you more than there."

She laughed. "Well, maybe that means you have two homes instead of one."

"You know? I kind of like the sound of that," he said with a smile. Outside at the SUV he turned to her. "I really like the sound of that."

She slipped her arms around his neck. "Good. Because what we have has nothing to do with the job. It has nothing to do with all the pain and headache I went through because of Larry and Warren. It has nothing to do with Tracy and the wonderful relationship we both had with her. It has to do with us. And I, for one, don't want to lose it."

"And I don't want to lose you," he said, his voice low. "So I highly suggest we play it by ear and see which place we want to live in. For the moment we won't change anything. You can spend some time with me at the compound, and I'll spend some time with you in Houston at your apartment. And then we can decide which place works better for us."

She snuggled into his shoulder and teased, "Are you sure you don't want a relationship just to get your hands on that VR system first?"

He pulled her closer and held her tight. "If that's a side benefit, who am I to argue?"

She rolled her eyes. "You get to play the hero in virtual and real life."

"As long as I'm your hero," he whispered, "I'm a happy man."

Epilogue

T O SEE MICHAEL and Tyson happy, with an air of
contentment on their faces, excited at the new beginning in their lives, well … Jace didn't know what to say.
He'd watched it happen—for Tyson at least—and Jace was
so damn happy for his buddy.

Tyson had been to hell and back. He'd been broken,
but, in true Tyson form, he hadn't stayed broken.

So how did Jace move forward? He'd been here at Legendary Security's compound for just over a week, and several
jobs were coming but hadn't commenced yet. Jace felt like
he was wasting Levi's time—and his own. Except being here
with his friends all in one place was an incredible experience,
and he wanted to keep that. Build on that. He could put
down roots here—maybe.

He felt like he had yet to prove himself. As if he'd been
given this position on the grace of others' recommendations.
But, so far, not having proven his worth.

And that fostered a fake-sick feeling in his stomach. Pity
was not his strong point. He could do a lot but hadn't
specialized in anything since leaving the military. He'd
worked at a lot of things, but nothing had been a good fit for
him.

He'd spent time on Rory's ranch, helping him and his
family out. Rory was another of his unit who'd walked out of

the military at his side. Having a reason to go and help had been a Godsend. Throwing hay bales and wielding a pitchfork had done wonders for working off the frustration Jace had been ignoring. But when the ranch work calmed down, he'd known it was time for him to leave.

But now he was here at Michael's recommendation. And Michael had been right. This was a good place. It did feel right. Just didn't feel like Jace's place. At least not yet. Jace knew, or knew of, most of the men in this room, but so many women—stunning, nice women—were in the room that he was blindsided.

"Are you okay?" Kai asked, appearing beside him. She had a bright smile on her face. Then she always did. And, if her smile was that much brighter for being with Tyson, well, Jace couldn't blame her.

He nodded. "Any reason I wouldn't be?"

She laughed. "Who knows? Like Tyson, you tend to sit in the background and watch everyone."

"I'm not that bad. Besides, I'm the new guy. It'll take a little while to find my place."

"It might. And it might not. Tyson was a new guy too." She motioned to the sprawling crowd. "I'm still finding my place as well."

"I can see that." Jace conceded that point to her. She was the latest in the group of women to arrive. Like he was the latest in the men. He had to admit, turning the page to a new start in his life held a lot of appeal right now.

Merk walked over and smacked Jace on his shoulder. "So are you ready?"

Jace raised an eyebrow. "Ready for what?"

"To lose your single status."

"Like that'll happen anytime soon." Jace waved to the

full room around him. "All the women are spoken for."

Ice laughed from behind him.

He turned and grinned. "Am I wrong?"

"Nope, you're not wrong." She shot him a wicked grin. "But wait until tomorrow. Your world is about to change."

"Says who?"

"Me. I spoke with Emily Leacock today, then did my research. You wait and see if I'm wrong. That voice of hers…"

In spite of himself, Jace was interested. "I don't know her. When is she coming?"

"First thing tomorrow." She stood taller to kiss his cheek. "Say goodbye to bachelorhood."

And she walked from the room, leaving Merk and Kai laughing like fools.

"I'll make my own decision," he declared to Ice's back. "Besides," Jace said, facing Merk and Kai, "the poor woman could already be married."

"Not if Ice did her homework." Kai snickered. "Ice's intuition is becoming legendary."

Jace smiled at that, given the name of the company Ice and Levi had pulled together. *Tomorrow, huh?* Well, he couldn't wait.

This concludes Book 10 of Heroes for Hire:
Tyson's Treasure.
Read about Jace's Jewel: Heroes for Hire, Book 11

Heroes for Hire: Jace's Jewel (Book #11)

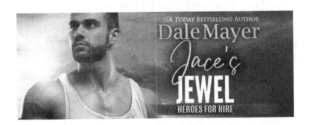

Members of a search-and-rescue team die in an accident. Not long later, others from the team are murdered. Jace is ordered by Legendary Securities to sort out the suspicious deaths.

Emily enjoys working for a large insurance company…until she's given several cases involving the same family. She finds an intimate connection with males in that family, and, afraid too much is going on in the background, she hires Legendary Securities.

As the investigation develops, more bodies turn up. Evidence of jealousy, greed and insurance payouts that shouldn't have been dispersed come to light. Emily pairs up with sexy Jace to delve into twisted, personal cases that may lead to even more murders if they don't figure this out…fast.

Book 11 is available now!

To find out more visit Dale Mayer's website.

dalemayer.com/jaces-jewel

Other Military Series by Dale Mayer

SEALs of Honor

Heroes for Hire

SEALs of Steel

The K9 Files

The Mavericks

Bullards Battle

Hathaway House

Terkel's Team

Ryland's Reach: Bullard's Battle (Book #1)

Welcome to a new stand-alone but interconnected series from Dale Mayer. This is Bullard's story—and that of his team's. All raw, rough, incredibly capable men who have one goal: to find out who was behind the attack on their leader, before the attacker, or attackers, return to finish the job.

Stay tuned for more nonstop action as the men narrow down their suspects ... and find a way to let love back into their own empty lives.

His rescue from the ocean after a horrible plane explosion was his top priority, in any way, shape, or form. A small sailboat and a nurse to do the job was more than Ryland hoped for.

When Tabi somehow drags him and his buddy Garret onboard and surprisingly gets them to a naval ship close by, Ryland figures he'd used up all his luck and his friend's too. Sure enough, those who attacked the plane they were in weren't content to let him slowly die in the ocean. No. Surviving had made him a target all over again.

Tabi isn't expecting her sailing holiday to include the rescue of two badly injured men and then to end with the loss of her beloved sailboat. Her instincts save them, but now she finds it tough to let them go—even as more of Bullard's team members come to them—until it becomes apparent that not only are Bullard and his men still targets … but she is too.

B ULLARD CHECKED THAT the helicopter was loaded with their bags and that his men were ready to leave.

He walked back one more time, his gaze on Ice. She'd never looked happier, never looked more perfect. His heart ached, but he knew she remained a caring friend and always would be. He opened his arms; she ran into them, and he held her close, whispering, "The offer still stands."

She leaned back and smiled up at him. "Maybe if and when Levi's been gone for a long enough time for me to forget," she said in all seriousness.

"That's not happening. You two, now three, will live long and happy lives together," he said, smiling down at the woman knew to be the most beautiful, inside and out. She would never be his, but he always kept a little corner of his heart open and available, in case she wanted to surprise him and to slide inside.

And then he realized she'd already been a part of his heart all this time. That was a good ten to fifteen years by now. But she kept herself in the friend category, and he understood because she and Levi, partners and now parents, were perfect together.

Bullard reached out and shook Levi's hand. "It was a hell of a blast," he said. "When you guys do a big splash, you really do a *big* splash."

Ice laughed. "A few days at home sounds perfect for me now."

"It looks great," he said, his hands on his hips as he surveyed the people in the massive pool surrounded by the palm trees, all designed and decked out by Ice. Right beside all the war machines that he heartily approved of. He grinned at her. "When are you coming over to visit?" His gaze went to Levi, raising his eyebrows back at her. "You guys should come over for a week or two or three."

"It's not a bad idea," Levi said. "We could use a long holiday, just not yet."

"That sounds familiar." Bullard grinned. "Anyway, I'm off. We'll hit the airport and then pick up the plane and head home." He added, "As always, call if you need me."

Everybody raised a hand as he returned to the helicopter and his buddy who was flying him to the airport. Ice had volunteered to shuttle him there, but he hadn't wanted to take her away from her family or to prolong the goodbye. He hopped inside, waving at everybody as the helicopter lifted. Two of his men, Ryland and Garret, were in the back seats. They always traveled with him.

Bullard would pick up the rest of his men in Australia. He stared down at the compound as he flew overhead. He preferred his compound at home, but damn they'd done a nice job here.

With everybody on the ground screaming goodbye, Bullard sailed over Houston, heading toward the airport. His two men never said a word. They all knew how he felt about Ice. But not one of them would cross that line and say anything. At least not if they expected to still have jobs.

It was one thing to fall in love with another man's woman, but another thing to fall in love with a woman who was so unique, so different, and so absolutely perfect that you knew, just knew, there was no hope of finding anybody else like her. But she and Levi had been together way before Bullard had ever met her, which made it that much more heartbreaking.

Still, he'd turned and looked forward. He had a full roster of jobs himself to focus on when he got home. Part of him was tired of the life; another part of him couldn't wait to head out on the next adventure. He managed to run everything from his command centers in one or two of his locations. He'd spent a lot of time and effort at the second one and kept a full team at both locations, yet preferred to spend most of his time at the old one. It felt more like home to him, and he'd like to be there now, but still had many more days before that could happen.

The helicopter lowered to the tarmac, he stepped out, said his goodbyes and walked across to where his private plane waited. It was one of the things that he loved, being a pilot of both helicopters and airplanes, and owning both birds himself.

That again was another way he and Ice were part of the same team, of the same mind-set. He'd been looking for another woman like Ice for himself, but no such luck. Sure, lots were around for short-term relationships, but most of them couldn't handle his lifestyle or the violence of the world that he lived in. He understood that.

The ones who did had a hard edge to them that he found difficult to live with. Bullard appreciated everybody's being alert and aware, but if there wasn't some softness in the women, they seemed to turn cold all the way through.

As he boarded his small plane, Ryland and Garret following behind, Bullard called out in his loud voice, "Let's go, slow pokes. We've got a long flight ahead of us."

The men grinned, confident Bullard was teasing, as was his usual routine during their off-hours.

"Well, we're ready, not sure about you though ..." Ryland said, smirking.

"We're waiting on you this time," Garret added with a chuckle. "Good thing you're the boss."

Bullard grinned at his two right-hand men. "Isn't that the truth?" He dropped his bags at one of the guys' feet and said, "Stow all this stuff, will you? I want to get our flight path cleared and get the hell out of here."

They'd all enjoyed the break. He tried to get over once a year to visit Ice and Levi and same in reverse. But it was time to get back to business. He started up the engines, got confirmation from the tower. They were heading to Australia for this next job. He really wanted to go straight back to Africa, but it would be a while yet. They'd refuel in Honolulu.

Ryland came in and sat down in the copilot's spot, buckled in, then asked, "You ready?"

Bullard laughed. "When have you ever known me *not* to be ready?" At that, he taxied down the runway. Before long he was up in the air, at cruising level, and heading to Hawaii. "Gotta love these views from up here," Bullard said. "This place is magical."

"It is once you get up above all the smog," he said. "Why Australia again?"

"Remember how we were supposed to check out that newest compound in Australia that I've had my eye on? Besides the alpha team is coming off that ugly job in Sydney. We'll give them a day or two of R&R then head home."

"Right. We could have some equally ugly payback on that job."

Bullard shrugged. "That goes for most of our jobs. It's the life."

"And don't you have enough compounds to look after?"

"Yes I do, but that kid in me still looks to take over the world. Just remember that."

"Better you go home to Africa and look after your first two compounds," Ryland said.

"Maybe," Bullard admitted. "But it seems hard to not continue expanding."

"You need a partner," Ryland said abruptly. "That might ease the savage beast inside. Keep you home more."

"Well, the only one I like," he said, "is married to my best friend."

"I'm sorry about that," Ryland said quietly. "What a shit deal."

"No," Bullard said. "I came on the scene last. They were always meant to be together. Especially now they are a family."

"If you say so," Ryland said.

Bullard nodded. "Damn right, I say so."

And that set the tone for the next many hours. They landed in Hawaii, and while they fueled up everybody got off to stretch their legs by walking around outside a bit as this was a small private airstrip, not exactly full of hangars and tourists. Then they hopped back on board again for takeoff.

"I can fly," Ryland offered as they took off.

"We'll switch in a bit," Bullard said. "Surprisingly, I'm doing okay yet, but I'll let you take her down."

"Yeah, it's still a long flight," Ryland said studying the islands below. It was a stunning view of the area.

"I love the islands here. Sometimes I just wonder about the benefit of, you know, crashing into the sea, coming up on a deserted island, and finding the simple life again," Bullard said with a laugh.

"I hear you," Ryland said. "Every once in a while, I wonder the same."

Several hours later Ryland looked up and said abruptly, "We've made good time considering we've already passed Fiji."

Bullard yawned.

"Let's switch."

Bullard smiled, nodded, and said, "Fine. I'll hand it over to you."

Just then a funny noise came from the engine on the right side.

They looked at each other, and Ryland said, "Uh-oh. That's not good news."

Boom!

And the plane exploded.

Find Bullard's Battle (Book #1) here!

To find out more visit Dale Mayer's website.

smarturl.it/DMSRyland

Damon's Deal: Terkel's Team (Book #1)

Welcome to a brand-new connected series of intrigue, betrayal, and … murder, from the *USA Today* best-selling author Dale Mayer. A series with all the elements you've come to love, plus so much more… including psychics!

A betrayal from within has Terkel frantic to protect those he can, as his team falls one by one, from a murderous killer he helped create.

ICE POURED HERSELF a coffee and sat down at the compound's massive dining room table with the others. When her phone rang, she smiled at the number displayed. "Hey, Terk. How're you doing?" She put the call on Speakerphone.

"I'm okay," Terkel said, his voice distracted and tight.

"Terk?" Merk called from across the table. He got up and walked closer and sat across from Levi. "You don't sound too good, brother. What's up?"

"I'm fine," Terk said. "Or I will be. Right now, things are blown to shit."

"As in literally?" Merk asked.

"The entire group," Terk said, "they're all gone. I had a solid team of eight, and they're all gone."

"Dead?"

Several others stood to join them, gathered around Ice's phone. Levi stepped forward, his hand on Ice's shoulder. "Terk? Are they all dead?"

"No." Terk took a deep breath. "I'm not making sense. I'm sorry."

"Take it easy," Ice said, her voice calm and reassuring. "What do you mean, *they're all gone?*"

"All their abilities are gone," he said. "Something's happened to them. Somebody has deliberately removed whatever super senses they could utilize—or what we have been utilizing for the last ten years for the government." His tone was bitter. "When the US gov recently closed us down, they promised that our black ops department would never rise again, but I didn't expect them to attack us personally."

"What are you talking about?" Merk said in alarm, standing up now to stare at Ice's phone. "Are you in danger?"

"Maybe? I don't know," Terk said. "I need to find out exactly what the hell's going on."

"What can we do to help?" Ice asked.

Terk gave a broken laugh. "That's not why I'm calling. Well, it is, but it isn't."

Ice looked at Merk, who frowned, as he shook his head. Ice knew he and the others had heard Terk's stressed out tone and the completely confusing bits and pieces coming from his mouth. Ice said, "Terk, you're not making sense again. Take a breath and explain. Please. You're scaring me."

Terk took a long slow deep breath. "Tell Stone to open the gate," he said. "She's out there."

"Who's out there?" Levi asked, hopped up, looked outside, and shrugged.

"She's coming up the road now. You have to let her in."

"Who? Why?"

"*Because*," he said, "she's also harnessed with C-4."

"Jesus," Levi said, bolting to display the camera feeds to the big screen in the room. "Is it live?"

"It is, and she's been sent to you."

"Well, that's an interesting move," Ice said, her voice sharp, activating her comm to connect to Stone in the control room. "Who's after us?"

"I think it's rebels within the Iranian government. But it could be our own government. I don't know anymore," Terk snapped. "I also don't know how they got her so close to you. Or how they pinned your connection to me," he said. "I've been very careful."

"We can look after ourselves," Ice said immediately. "But who is this woman to you?"

"She's pregnant," he said, "so that adds to the intensity here."

"Understood. So who is the father? Is he connected somehow?"

There was silence on the other end.

Merk said, "Terk, talk to us."

"She's carrying my baby," Terk replied, his voice heavy.

Merk, his expression grim, looked at Ice, her face mirroring his shock. He asked, "How do you know her, Terk?"

"Brother, you don't understand," Terk said. "I've never met this woman before in my life." And, with that, the phone went dead.

Find Terkel's Team (Book #1) here!

To find out more visit Dale Mayer's website.

smarturl.it/DMSTTDamon

Author's Note

Thank you for reading Tyson's Treasure: Heroes for Hire, Book 10! If you enjoyed the book, please take a moment and leave a short review.

Dear reader,

I love to hear from readers, and you can contact me at my website: www.dalemayer.com or at my Facebook author page. To be informed of new releases and special offers, sign up for my newsletter or follow me on BookBub. And if you are interested in joining Dale Mayer's Reader Group, here is the Facebook sign up page.
https://smarturl.it/DaleMayerFBGroup

Cheers,
Dale Mayer

Your THREE Free Books
Are Waiting!

Grab your copy of SEALs of Honor Books 1 – 3 for free!

Meet Mason, Hawk and Dane. *Brave, badass warriors who serve their country with honor and love their women to the limits of life and death.*

DOWNLOAD your copy right now! Just tell me where to send it.
www.smarturl.it/DaleHonorFreeBundle

About the Author

Dale Mayer is a *USA Today* best-selling author, best known for her SEALs military romances, her Psychic Visions series, and her Lovely Lethal Garden cozy series. Her contemporary romances are raw and full of passion and emotion (Broken But ... Mending series). Her thrillers will keep you guessing (By Death series), and her romantic comedies will keep you giggling (*It's a Dog's Life*, a stand-alone novella; and the Broken Protocols series, starring Charming Marvin, the cat).

Dale honors the stories that come to her—and some of them are crazy and break all the rules and cross multiple genres!

To go with her fiction, she also writes nonfiction in many different fields, with books available on résumé writing, companion gardening, and the US mortgage system. She has recently published her Career Essentials series. All her books are available in print and ebook format.

Connect with Dale Mayer Online

Dale's Website – www.dalemayer.com
Twitter – @DaleMayer
Facebook – facebook.com/DaleMayer.author
BookBub – bookbub.com/authors/dale-mayer

Also by Dale Mayer

Published Adult Books:

Bullard's Battle

Ryland's Reach, Book 1

Cain's Cross, Book 2

Eton's Escape, Book 3

Garret's Gambit, Book 4

Kano's Keep, Book 5

Fallon's Flaw, Book 6

Quinn's Quest, Book 7

Bullard's Beauty, Book 8

Bullard's Best, Book 9

Terkel's Team

Damon's Deal, Book 1

Kate Morgan

Simon Says... Hide, Book 1

Hathaway House

Aaron, Book 1

Brock, Book 2

Cole, Book 3

Denton, Book 4

The K9 Files

Harley, Book 14

The K9 Files, Books 1–2

The K9 Files, Books 3–4

The K9 Files, Books 5–6

The K9 Files, Books 7–8

The K9 Files, Books 9–10

The K9 Files, Books 11–12

Lovely Lethal Gardens

Arsenic in the Azaleas, Book 1

Bones in the Begonias, Book 2

Corpse in the Carnations, Book 3

Daggers in the Dahlias, Book 4

Evidence in the Echinacea, Book 5

Footprints in the Ferns, Book 6

Gun in the Gardenias, Book 7

Handcuffs in the Heather, Book 8

Ice Pick in the Ivy, Book 9

Jewels in the Juniper, Book 10

Killer in the Kiwis, Book 11

Lifeless in the Lilies, Book 12

Murder in the Marigolds, Book 13

Lovely Lethal Gardens, Books 1–2

Lovely Lethal Gardens, Books 3–4

Lovely Lethal Gardens, Books 5–6

Lovely Lethal Gardens, Books 7–8

Lovely Lethal Gardens, Books 9–10

Psychic Vision Series

Tuesday's Child

Hide 'n Go Seek

Maddy's Floor

Garden of Sorrow

Knock Knock...

Rare Find

Eyes to the Soul

Now You See Her

Shattered

Into the Abyss

Seeds of Malice

Eye of the Falcon

Itsy-Bitsy Spider

Unmasked

Deep Beneath

From the Ashes

Stroke of Death

Ice Maiden

Snap, Crackle...

Psychic Visions Books 1–3

Psychic Visions Books 4–6

Psychic Visions Books 7–9

By Death Series

Touched by Death

Haunted by Death

Chilled by Death

By Death Books 1–3

Broken Protocols – Romantic Comedy Series

Cat's Meow

Cat's Pajamas

Cat's Cradle

Cat's Claus

Broken Protocols 1-4

Broken and... Mending

Skin

Scars

Scales (of Justice)

Broken but... Mending 1-3

Glory

Genesis

Tori

Celeste

Glory Trilogy

Biker Blues

Morgan: Biker Blues, Volume 1

Cash: Biker Blues, Volume 2

SEALs of Honor

Mason: SEALs of Honor, Book 1

Hawk: SEALs of Honor, Book 2

Dane: SEALs of Honor, Book 3

Swede: SEALs of Honor, Book 4

Shadow: SEALs of Honor, Book 5

Cooper: SEALs of Honor, Book 6

Heroes for Hire

Heroes for Hire, Books 10–12

Heroes for Hire, Books 13–15

SEALs of Steel

Badger: SEALs of Steel, Book 1

Erick: SEALs of Steel, Book 2

Cade: SEALs of Steel, Book 3

Talon: SEALs of Steel, Book 4

Laszlo: SEALs of Steel, Book 5

Geir: SEALs of Steel, Book 6

Jager: SEALs of Steel, Book 7

The Final Reveal: SEALs of Steel, Book 8

SEALs of Steel, Books 1–4

SEALs of Steel, Books 5–8

SEALs of Steel, Books 1–8

The Mavericks

Kerrick, Book 1

Griffin, Book 2

Jax, Book 3

Beau, Book 4

Asher, Book 5

Ryker, Book 6

Miles, Book 7

Nico, Book 8

Keane, Book 9

Lennox, Book 10

Gavin, Book 11

Shane, Book 12

Diesel, Book 13

Jerricho, Book 14

The Mavericks, Books 1–2

The Mavericks, Books 3–4

The Mavericks, Books 5–6

The Mavericks, Books 7–8

The Mavericks, Books 9–10

The Mavericks, Books 11–12

Collections

Dare to Be You...

Dare to Love...

Dare to be Strong...

RomanceX3

Standalone Novellas

It's a Dog's Life

Riana's Revenge

Second Chances

Published Young Adult Books:

Family Blood Ties Series

Vampire in Denial

Vampire in Distress

Vampire in Design

Vampire in Deceit

Vampire in Defiance

Vampire in Conflict

Vampire in Chaos

Vampire in Crisis

Vampire in Control

Vampire in Charge

Family Blood Ties Set 1–3

Family Blood Ties Set 1–5

Family Blood Ties Set 4–6

Family Blood Ties Set 7–9

Sian's Solution, A Family Blood Ties Series Prequel Novelette

Design series

Dangerous Designs

Deadly Designs

Darkest Designs

Design Series Trilogy

Standalone

In Cassie's Corner

Gem Stone (a Gemma Stone Mystery)

Time Thieves

Published Non-Fiction Books:

Career Essentials

Career Essentials: The Résumé

Career Essentials: The Cover Letter

Career Essentials: The Interview

Career Essentials: 3 in 1

Made in the USA
Las Vegas, NV
18 March 2022

45914810R00134